Clare Atkins wrote her first book, *Nona & Me*, while living in Arnhem Land, and is now based in Darwin. *Nona & Me* won the 2016 Book of the Year in the NT Literary Awards, was an Honour Book in the 2015 Children's Book Council of Australia Awards, and was longlisted for the 2015 Inky Awards and highly commended for the 2015 Victorian Premier's Literary Awards. She has worked as a scriptwriter on many successful television series including *All Saints*, *Home and Away*, *Winners & Losers* and *Wonderland*.

Winner, Book of the Year

[illegible] Northern Territory Literary Awards

PRAISE FOR *NONA & ME* BY CLARE ATKINS

Honour Book, 2015 Children's Book Council of Australia, Book of the Year for Older Readers

Winner, Book of the Year: 2016 Northern Territory Literary Awards

Highly commended, 2015 Victorian Premier's Literary Awards

Longlisted, 2015 Inky Awards

'A powerful coming-of-age story ... Atkins writes with clear-eyed sensitivity ... *Nona & Me* is poignant young-adult fiction invoking the complex and often overlooked realities of remote indigenous life.'
– *Sydney Morning Herald*

'Clare Atkins writes about a place and a time with love and care, and explores a complicated and fraught situation with honesty and respect ... *Nona & Me* is one of those wonderful books that takes you deeply into a rarely seen world and brings it vibrantly to life.'
– *Books + Publishing*

'A powerful, beautifully contoured story of cross-cultural friendship.'
– *The Weekend Australian*

'[Clare Atkins] wrestles with some of this country's most hotly debated political issues with a rare lightness of touch ... a convincing portrait of a naive but feverish first love, friendships waxing and waning, and the clash between fitting in and sticking to your values. Above all, there's a warmth and optimism that's hard to resist.'
– *Sunday Age*

'Clare Atkins delivers a polished, unflinching book that deserves to be read'
– *The Age*

'A thought-provoking debut'
– *The West Australian*

'Clare Atkins' debut novel is a triumph: a coming-of-age tale that celebrates friendship and loyalty, family and community. Here is a striking new voice in Australian youth literature, and her story is one that will surely leave its mark.'
– *Kill Your Darlings*

'Atkins has chosen difficult terrain for her first novel and mapped it with honesty, style and insight.'
– *Adelaide Advertiser*

'A fascinating book, beautifully told, with rich insight into a deeply Australian but little known community.'
– Jackie French AM

'Rosie's story brims with the joy and pain and complexity of friendship and love at sixteen. I adored this smart, heartfelt book about family, kinship, country, and finding out what really matters.'
– Fiona Wood

Between Us

Between Us

CLARE ATKINS

Published by Black Inc.,
an imprint of Schwartz Publishing Pty Ltd
Level 1, 221 Drummond Street
Carlton VIC 3053, Australia
enquiries@blackincbooks.com
www.blackincbooks.com

9781760640217 (paperback)
9781743820216 (ebook)

A catalogue record for this
book is available from the
National Library of Australia

Cover design by Tristan Main
Text design and typesetting by Marilyn de Castro

Printed in Australia by McPherson's Printing Group.

ANA

I start again.

I lift my right foot off the ground, and place it on the lowest step of the bus. My nerves are an electric lightning storm inside me, fraught and fiery.

The officer waves for me to get on. Her voice cracks with impatience. 'Hurry up!'

I lift my other foot. Nothing happens. The officer doesn't yell or grab me or shove me forwards.

I take another step, then one more. I'm up in the aisle now. Zahra beckons me towards her, but she's already sitting next to Jamileh; there's no room for me there. The boys are up the back of the bus – I can't sit with them either. Zahra indicates the empty seat in front of her, and I slide into it, as another officer starts calling the roll. This one is short and Asian, with a clipped, singsong way of talking.

'ADE036.'

A muttered 'yes' and a shuffle from the back.

'COR005.'

'Yes.' Zahra's voice, bold and grinning behind me.

'KIN016.'

Silence. He tries again. 'KIN016? Is that you?' He's looking at me.

I manage a small nod. The lightning flashes inside me again.

He ticks me off the list, hurries through the rest of the numbers, then turns to the bus driver. 'Good to go.'

The roller door in front of us screeches open, and the bus eases forwards. It stops just a few metres in front of where we were; there's a second roller door blocking our way. The one behind us closes, and for a moment we are locked in a concrete void that is neither in nor out. My stomach churns.

Then the outer door clunks upwards and the bus lurches out onto the driveway. The Asian officer hurries to take a seat beside the female officer, just in front of me.

The bus slows at a boom gate. The final barrier is raised. Then we're out on an empty road. Smooth black bitumen, painted with a carefully dotted white line straight down the middle. The land around us seems to stretch forever, an expanse of flat red earth. The trees on the roadside are stringy, with leaves like bursts of green fireworks erupting into the clear blue sky. So much green, so much space, and not a single person or building in sight. It's the opposite of home.

We pass a section of blackened trees, burnt trunks standing like charred sentinels guarding the way to the city.

Then we're on a bridge zooming across a shimmering body of water. The ocean, vast and endless. The memory of terror grips me and twists my guts into a knot. I gasp.

The Asian officer turns to face me, misreading my panic. 'First day?'

My nod is as small and fragile as the wings of a butterfly flapping.

He says, 'No need to be scared. You'll like it.' His voice softens even more, as he adds, 'It's a nice school. My son goes there.'

I can't hide my surprise.

He smiles, and his dark eyes crease into triangles. 'His name's Jonathan. He's in Year 10. You see him, you tell him his dad says to help you, okay? If you need anything.' He holds his lanyard up above the back of the seat and says, 'This is me.'

I see his ID photo and his name: Kenny Do.

The female officer nudges him, and he turns back to face the front. I study him from behind. He has thick black hair, clipped carefully in around his ears. His uniform is wrinkled around the shoulders, as if someone only ironed the flat bits. His wife, I suppose.

I've seen him in our compound before; he's one of the good officers, Zahra says.

I silently practise the names I need to remember. Strange sounds. New words.

Kenny Do.

Jonathan.

JONO

I wake,
smog in my head.
Heart like lead.
Reluctantly
swing the soles
of my feet
to touch the tiles.
See it's eight.
Already late.
Want to text Will,
then remember I can't.
Last night,
smoking with the boys,
choking on dumb jokes
and guffaws.
Time suspended.
Skating home in the dark.
Dad on the moulting velvet couch,
holding the remote control,
(carefully bound in cling wrap
to preserve it from the elements).
Watching *The Godfather*.
(A burnt DVD he bought for a dollar.)
He looks up, voice hard.
'Where you been, Jonathan?'
I hate that name.
'Come here.'
I take a step closer.

Look him in the eyes,
let him see the red cracks in mine;
fault lines above hell.
'You been drinking?
Or smoking again?'
I shrug.
Too
stoned
to
string
words
together
to
make
a
sentence.
His eyes flare. 'Why you do this?
Waste your time on stupid things?'
He uses the only real power he has:
'Give me your phone.'
I slump into a groan,
know from experience he won't budge.
I place
my friends
my games
my music
my life
into his hand.
He looks triumphant.
'One week.'

Seven days stretch
before me,
black and endless.
I force myself to stand
and start the day.

ANA

My eyes drink in our surroundings as we fly past. A cluster of red roofs, hiding amongst lush green trees. Powerlines so big they're like wire skipping ropes held up in the air by metal giants.

We seem to be skirting a town now; one side of the road is still bush, but the other is a high mound of dirt that dips away. Beyond that, fences block our view of sprawling backyards.

Zahra leans forwards in her seat, explaining in Farsi: 'That's Palmerston. They have a cinema there.'

Jamileh's eyes widen. 'How do you know?'

Zahra says, 'I've been on excursions there. A few times.'

Zahra's been here almost two years; if anyone wants to know anything they ask her.

Palmerston flickers past us like a suburban mirage. We don't drive in.

More bush and wide roads give way to a barricade of houses. These ones are surrounded by high wire fences, shrouded in black fabric that glints in the sun. Enormous shiny cars zoom past us in both directions.

Then suddenly we're climbing off the bus. I stay close to Zahra and Jamileh. The high school, at least, feels vaguely familiar; from the front, it is a series of concrete buildings. Most are low set, but there is one that is like an apartment block, at least three storeys high.

There is a woman waiting to greet us. She's wearing a beautiful, long, flowing skirt covered in red flowers, and dangly golden earrings drip from her ears. She welcomes Jamileh, then turns to me. 'And you must be Anahita.'

I think KIN016. But I nod.

'I'm Lisa. I work in the Intensive English Centre. I'll be looking after you both.'

'Me too, Miss,' says Zahra.

Lisa smiles. 'Looks like you've already got a friend. That's great. Thanks, Zahra.'

Zahra gives her a cheeky grin. 'No worries, Miss.'

Her words sound strange and round. *Is she speaking Australian?* Zahra sees my surprised expression and flicks me a wink. Lisa leads the way into the school. There's an enormous grass courtyard in front of us, but instead of crossing it we turn into the tall building and begin to climb a flight of stairs.

Lisa says, 'The Intensive English Centre's on the top floor. So it's easy to find us if you ever get lost.'

The stairwell folds back on itself in concrete zigzags as we ascend. A group of girls overtake us, chatting, happy and carefree; I long to be like them so much it aches. Two boys run up the stairs, taking them two at a time. Further up, there's a boy and girl with their arms snaked around each other's waists; I try not to stare.

We reach the top. The windows are full of bursting blue sky. There is no smog at all.

I snap back to attention as Lisa pushes a door open and waves us through to an office. We're introduced to a woman called Farah, who works as cultural liaison. She smiles and tells us in careful, slow-spoken English that she's Iranian too. We talk briefly about where our families are from, then Jamileh moves off with Farah, to be shown around. I'm relieved that Zahra stays with me.

Lisa points out the various classrooms, then hands me a piece of paper showing a grid filled with words. 'This is your timetable. It tells you which class you have when. Your records say your English is quite good. You learnt in Iran – is that right? And a little bit on Christmas Island, once the school started?'

I say, 'Yes.'

'Nothing on Nauru?' I shake my head. 'We've put you in the "Developing English" phase.'

'Same as me.' Zahra gives me an encouraging smile.

Lisa says, 'That means you have three lines of Intensive English up here then three lines downstairs with the mainstream classes.'

'Lines are classes,' Zahra explains.

'What is mainstream?' I ask.

'Classes with the Australian students.' I give her a small, nervous smile. Lisa quickly adds, 'Everyone's very friendly, don't worry. And we can put you in the same Maths and Humanities classes as Zahra, if you like.'

'Yes. Thank you.'

'No worries.' Those words again. 'Then you just have to

choose an elective. Do you think you'd like to study Science, Technology, Sport or Art?'

I don't even have to think about it. 'Science, please.'

Zahra says, 'I'm in Art.'

But I'm decided. I think of all the books in Baba's study, piled high. A shiver of anticipation runs through me.

Lisa's warm brown eyes search out mine. 'Anahita? Are you feeling okay? Any problems just come and see me, alright? I'm always here.'

I nod and – impulsively – form my lips around the strange words: 'No wor-ries-miss.'

Lisa laughs and holds a single thumb up. 'Great.'

KENNY

We're halfway back to the detention centre before Cara brings it up. 'Shouldn't have done that, by the way.'

'Sorry. What?' I turn to look at her.

'Shouldn't have told that girl about your son.'

'Oh. Right.' I've only been in the job a few months; the other officers seem to love giving us newbies advice.

Sure enough, Cara continues, 'Last thing you want is your kid getting mixed up with someone like that.'

I have to laugh. She clearly doesn't know Jonathan. 'Someone *like that*? She's probably better behaved than my son. He's no angel, believe me.'

Cara doesn't even crack a smile. 'That makes it even worse. They can use your kids against you. Manipulate you. Manipulate him.' She must see the scepticism in my expression, because she adds, 'I learnt the hard way. Became friends with a few of the detainees on Facebook last year. One of their husbands saw pictures of my daughter. And every time I saw him after that he'd say stuff like: "Your daughter is very beautiful." It was creepy, you know. Like a threat. I was so relieved when he got moved to another centre.'

There's a trill of fear in her voice, even now.

I want to reassure her.

I want to reassure myself.

I say, 'I'm not worried. My son can look after himself.'

JONO

I skate
from the cyclone fences
of the Narrows,
to the tiled porches
of Fannie Bay.
Kick stop,
lean my board
against the whitewashed wall.
Paste a smile on my lips
and head into Will's house.
Lean my arms on the cool marble bench.
Will's mum, Tracy, breezes around the kitchen
in tight black gym gear.
'Jono. French toast?'

'Like I ever say no.'
I sit next to Will.
The coins in my pocket
clink against the stool.
($2.50 from the back of Dad's couch.)
Tracy checks her Fitbit.
'Aren't you boys running late?
School's already started. I'd better drive you.'
Will groans. 'We were gonna skate.'
There's a thin line of maple syrup dribbling down his chin.
I say, 'We can chuck our boards in the car
and skate home after school.'
He rolls his eyes at me. 'Suck.'
I inhale breakfast, then follow him upstairs.
My feet drag on the floorboards.
Will watches with worried eyes.
'You alright?'
I try to justify my gloom:
'Dad took my phone again.'
He looks relieved.
'Is *that* all? Want my spare?'
He digs into a drawer,
pulls out the second latest iPhone and a charger,
and chucks them into my grappling hands.
'Lifesaver,' I say.
But my voice is flat.

ANA

I stay quiet and listen as the class talks in English around me. Some of their phrases are halting, some are broken, some flow. The teacher, Ms Vo, is leading a discussion about a book they've just started studying. It's called *The Outsiders*. It has a black-and-white cover with a photo of three clean-shaven white boys staring insolently at the camera, hair flopping into their faces.

I flip through the pages, and see words that are similar to ones I know but slightly different: *outa*, *talkin'*, *y'all*. I wonder if the words are Australian, like 'no worries'. There is swearing too; people telling each other to shut up.

Three boys up the back seem to like the book, or are at least interested in the language.

'Is blade "knife", Miss?'

'What is a "hood?" Someone stealing?'

'And what about "football"? Is it the round ball or the red one they use here?'

They get their answers from Ms Vo, then erupt in a babble of language I don't recognise.

Zahra grins and whispers in Farsi, 'They're Greek – they're always like this. I call them the Greek Chorus.'

Our class is small, just nine students including me. There is Zahra, Jamileh, a boy from Sierra Leone called Ibrahim, the Greek Chorus and two boys named Mohammed. I recognise one of them from the back of the bus.

The group is surprisingly supportive. When someone makes a mistake, no-one laughs, or not in a mean way at least.

'Anahita?'

I hear my name, but nothing else. Blood rushes to my head as Ms Vo repeats the question. She has kind eyes, short-cropped hair and a slim-fitting skirt.

'Anahita, did you want to ask about any of the words in chapter one?'

Her question hangs between us. I want to please her. I want to please her so much. I hear myself say, 'Yes.' Then nothing more. The words stick in my throat.

Jamileh nods her encouragement, and Zahra nudges me. Everyone is watching me, waiting.

A word leaps out from the page in front of me. I ask, 'What is ... Ponyboy?'

A few people laugh, but Ms Vo hushes them. 'Who can answer Anahita?'

One of the Mohammeds says, 'Ponyboy is his name. The name of ... main character.'

I ask, 'Is this ... Australian name?'

Ms Vo shakes her head. 'The book is set in America, and even there it's definitely not a common name. They call him Pony for short, as a nickname. Does everyone know that term: nickname? It's a short, made-up name, like how Pony calls his brother Darren, Darry. Has anyone here got a nickname?'

Both the Mohammeds say 'Mo' and then laugh.

The bell rings, and the students' smiles dissolve into hurried packing up.

Ms Vo raises her voice above the bustle. 'Everyone look up five more words that you don't know from chapter one tonight, please.'

I collect my things and consult my carefully folded piece of paper.

Zahra leans over to see. 'What have you got next?'

'Science.'

She frowns. 'Why didn't you choose Art? We could've been together the whole time.'

'Science is my favourite subject.'

'But you'll be alone.' She says it as if being alone is the world's most terrible thing, as if she hasn't been through far worse. 'I bet you could still change … or skip it today if you want …'

But I don't want to. I shake my head.

'Want me to walk you down there?' She's like a little mother shepherding me through my first day of school.

'I'll be okay.'

'Are you sure?'

I'm not sure at all. A class full of Australians. What if they ask me questions? Or laugh at my English? Or ignore me?

And how will I find the room? I check the timetable again. It says: *Mainstream. Room 2B.* What if I get lost? I picture myself floating in a sea of uniforms, all of them the same. The thought is both terrifying and exhilarating

I say, 'I'll see you after class.' I sound more confident than I feel.

I head towards the stairs, pausing to give Zahra one last wave. And then she's gone.

The concrete stairs swallow me as I descend.

The teacher welcomes me into the class with a beaming smile and introduces herself as Ms Turner. She tells me that her mother is Persian.

'Not that I speak the language,' she adds, apologetically. 'The only word I really know is my name: Pari. Fairy.'

A boy at the desk next to mine smirks, and I hear him whisper that Fairy is a gay name. I don't understand. I've always loved the name Pari. It suits her too; she's short and elfish and seems to float around the classroom, a secret light behind her eyes.

She explains that they are studying evolution, and someone called Darwin. Perhaps it is who this city is named after, I'm not sure.

Ms Turner presses a small remote control in her hand and a picture appears on the whiteboard at the front of the room: an ape, its hunched form gradually becoming more upright and less hairy as it walks across the screen until, in the last image, it is a human.

The chatter at the back of the room becomes sniggers. Ms Turner pauses mid-sentence, and I think she's going to yell, but then her eyes twinkle, as she says, 'Of course some of us are a little more evolved than others ... what do you think, Jono?'

Some students erupt into laughter. I follow Ms Turner's gaze and see a boy slouched at a table up the back of the room. His face is half hidden by a curtain of straight shoulder-length brown hair. He's wearing a long-sleeved black top under his uniform, despite the heat. It makes his body look thin and angular, jutting off his stool in sharp lines.

He mumbles, 'Guess so, Miss', and shoves his hair back from his face. It falls forwards again straight away.

Ms Turner says, more pointedly this time, 'I would really love it if you three could listen.' It's aimed at the boy – 'Jono' – and his two friends, a tall blond boy and a girl who seems to be dressed like a boy. They smirk at each other.

Jono scowls, but I'm not sure if it's at the teacher or his friends.

Ms Turner says, 'Maybe you can read the next paragraph for us, Jono.'

He shrugs, then starts to read.

His voice is softer than I imagined. I thought it would be harsh and angry; his body language seems to say: *Stay away*. But as he reads his voice becomes almost animated, like he's forgotten to be bored.

JONO

The new girl is staring at me.
Eyes, almost black,
flicker shy
up, down, then back.
Is there something in my teeth?
Can she see the zit on my neck?
I squirm in my seat.
Will grins. 'What have you got that I don't?'
(He's joking, of course.
It's always the other way around.)

'Send her a note.'
I aim a kick under the table.
Turner says, 'Jono, please.
Don't make me say your name again.'
I sneak another glance.
The girl's facing the front now.
The fabric wrapped around her head
cascades over her shoulder,
pooling on the desk below.
She senses my gaze and turns around again.
Dark brown eyes lock on mine.
Her gaze is curious,
unapologetic and strong,
like she knows herself;
maybe even knows me.
The corners of her lips bend into a curve.
Mine do too.
She makes me want to
sit up straighter,
get a (better) haircut,
catch my breath.
The bell rings.
She jumps up, alarmed.
(Pun intended. I do listen in English. Sometimes.)
Packs her books in a hurry.
Walks to the door
and suddenly
stops.
Skin
shrinking

by
the
second.
She takes
a slow step
into the corridor
then looks back
through the doorway
at me
– me! –
with a question in her eyes.

ANA

'There you are!' Zahra appears in the hallway and scoops me into a stroll. 'Was it okay?'

I nod, wishing she hadn't arrived quite so soon. I wanted to ask that boy if he is Kenny's son. The teacher called him Jono. She said it quite often, perhaps every ten minutes, a small crease appearing between her eyebrows each time. I'm almost sure it's him though. He looks like a stretched-out, sun-kissed version of his dad. His hair is lighter than Kenny's, his skin more tan and less yellow. But then he smiles, and those eyes, they're the same. Triangles of kind darkness.

I glance back down the hallway and see Jono exit the classroom. His blond friend, Not-Jonathan, is beside him. Not-Jonathan is paler, taller, musclier, green-eyed. His hair is swept across his forehead as if the wind blew it so hard in one direction that it got stuck there.

Not-Jonathan sees his friend looking at me, says something and laughs.

I remember twirling happily in my uniform this morning. Maman said I was beautiful, and Arash clapped his little hands. My grin took over my face as I stared at myself in the dull metal mirror in the bathroom. The uniform looked just like the ones the girls wear on Australian TV, and the thought delighted me: *I am one of them.*

But now, under the boys' gazes, a new thought surfaces: this second-hand uniform, this dress that the officer gave me last night, has probably been worn by other girls. Other girls like me. How long were they at this school? And where are they now?

Zahra is watching me, waiting. 'Anahita? More English now, yes?'

'Yes.' I breathe a little easier.

We turn the corner and start to climb the stairs back to the safety of higher ground. I link her arm in mine.

JONO

I think I see tongues.
Slippery pink eels darting in and out of dark mouth-caves.
I groan. 'Guys. Please. We're trying to eat.'
Mel laughs,
as she and Will
retract their body parts;

become separate entities again.
I take another bite of pie.
The oozing meat and sauce,
soft and sweet in my mouth.
(I'd eat ten if I could afford it.)
Will throws me a sheepish smile.
'You coming to mine this arvo, Nippy?'
'Dunno.'
Last year,
after school,
it was always the four of us.
But now it's just me
and them
and the memory of Priya,
pulling me down,
down,
down.
I elbow Ibrahim. 'What are you guys doing?'
He doesn't hear.
Too busy *Crushing Candy* with Mac.
I'd escape into that world too,
if I had my phone,
or Will's wasn't flat.
Will teases: 'Invite that new girl if you want.'
Mac's girl-radar goes up. 'What new girl?'
'Some chick was checking Jono out in Science.'
'Is she hot?'
Will says, 'Prob'ly. She was wearing one of those head things.'
'A hijab?'
'Isn't that the full-face one?'

'Nah, that's something else.'

We look to Ibrahim, our authority on all things Muslim, but he's lost in his digital crusade.

Mel frowns. 'Aren't Muslim girls really strict? Like, I don't think they're allowed to date.'

Will laughs. 'You're not either, according to your mum.'

I say, 'Doesn't matter anyway. I'm not interested.'

Mac grins. 'I might be. Reckon this girl's a *budju*?'

I shrug. 'She's alright.'

But her smile is still dancing in the corners of my eyes.

ANA

Our next class is in the library. I stare at the row upon row of clean, crisp-edged books. 'Are we allowed to take books … home?'

The word sounds strange and wrong. Home is my Baba's study and the smell of freshly cooked curry on the stove.

Zahra nods. 'You just put it through the metal detector.'

Jamileh attempts a sentence in English. 'How many … we can … take?'

Ms Vo overhears. 'We just have to sign you girls up to get library cards today. Then you can borrow whatever you like, for up to two weeks at a time.' She turns to me. 'Is there anything in particular you like reading, Anahita?'

I blush and look down. I'm a slow reader. One book in English can take me months. I know Zahra can read proper adult books in English, but I doubt Jamileh can. I make a mental note to ask her when no-one else is around.

To my relief, Ms Vo says, 'Maybe you could just borrow some picture books to start off. You have a little brother, don't you?'

I wonder how she knows. Are the teachers told everything? What else does she know about me?

I say, 'His name is Arash. He is three years old.'

'Perfect. You can read them to him then. He'll love it.'

I smile, grateful that she seems to understand.

KENNY

I'm on edge all morning, thinking of Cara's words. Surely she was exaggerating. The girl looked harmless. She couldn't have been more than fifteen years old. And the fear in her eyes: it was real. I'm sure of that.

I consider asking Raj about it, but the video camera's on. He's filming from the doorway as I search a Hazara family's room. I check all the usual hiding spots: under the mattress, in the covers, the drawers, the bathroom, the wardrobe.

I don't find any contraband. I'm glad. I don't want to have to write it up.

The pager sounds from my waist.

It's Cara. 'Kenny, where are you?'

'In Surf.'

'The school bus is leaving soon.'

'I'm not coming. I was just filling in this morning. Rick's going with you this arvo.'

She groans. 'What'd I do to deserve that?' She's only half joking; every officer in here knows Rick is a jerk. Wherever he's stationed there's a good chance there'll be some kind of trouble.

The pager clicks off.

Raj has the camera on pause now, so I take the chance to ask, 'Hey, do you ever talk to the detainees?'

'What do you mean by talk? Like hi, bye, how's it going? Sure.'

'No, more than that. Like, do you ever ask them about their lives? Or tell them about yours?'

Raj's thick black eyebrows furrow. 'Why would I do that? I'm not an idiot.'

My heart sinks.

JONO

I loiter after school,
near the main exit,
wondering if I'll see
the new girl from Science.
Does she catch the bus?
Or ride? Or walk?
P platers start their engines.
Students stream into waiting buses like ants.
Mel appears and punches me on the arm.
'So, you coming?'
'I'm thinking about it.'

'What if Will and I promise not to pash?'
She's always like that.
Direct. Some say blunt.
(But it's the blunt people who'd say blunt, right?)
'You waiting for your new girlfriend?' she teases.
I blush. 'Don't you start.'
'Maybe I can wait too.'
'Mel, please – go. I'll see you there.'
She says: 'Come.
We don't need Priya to have fun.'
Then, thankfully, starts walking away.
I scan the crowd again.
Then I see her,
bag heavy on her back.
She's flanked by the friend from this morning
and a tall white man.
Her dad?
Doubt it.
He's pale with a stern-set face.
Hair cropped close to his oddly rectangular head.
Phone clipped to a belt.
He stops and checks cards
– bus passes? –
as the kids climb on.
He ticks a list
then looks around.
My eyes drop to his T-shirt.
It's grey with a yellow circle embroidered on the chest.
The same one Dad puts on before his shifts.

ANA

Neither of the officers on the bus home are Kenny. Instead there is the woman from this morning and a brash white man everyone secretly calls Blockhead; his head is angular and his expression is always icy. Zahra says to avoid him.

He yells for us to 'Sit down, for Godsake!' then takes a seat up the front, as far away from us as possible. He nods to the driver. 'That's all of them. Let's go.'

The engine starts and the bus pulls away from the kerb. My eyes linger on the tall concrete buildings, students still swarming out the doors. Girls and boys, smiling and waving their goodbyes. Climbing into buses and cars as big as tanks. Stopping to hug and kiss, like they're not going to see each other for years.

And in the middle of it all I see the boy called Jono standing near the entrance to the school.

He's staring at our bus in something like confusion. Or shock. Or distaste.

His mouth is half open, like he's saying, 'Oh … you're one of them.'

My heart drops into my stomach.

Zahra looks over at me. 'You okay?'

I manage a nod. Then we're round the corner, and Jono and the school disappear.

But his expression stays lodged in my mind.

JONO

I tick-tack through the streets
past the turn-off to Will's.
I want to be alone,
so I head home.
Questions rattle 'round my skull.
So she's a detention kid ...
But what does that actually mean?
That she came on a boat?
Doesn't look like it to me.
She holds her head high,
meets your eye, has pride.
How long are they out there?
And why do they lock them up?
I try to remember what Dad's told me about his work.
But either I haven't been listening,
or he hasn't said much.
Probably both.
I glide across three lanes of Bagot Road.
A car horn blares indignation.
I give them the finger.
My board smacks into the gutter,
and I stagger forwards.
'Fuck!'

ANA

Security checks our bags. The female officer behind the desk has a lanyard that says Milly White. She has red hair that curls like flames licking at her ears. She heaves my backpack off the conveyor belt, and passes it back to me. 'What'd you do? Rob a bookstore?'

I tense. 'They are from library. My teacher say ...' I trail off as I see her grin.

She says, 'I'm joking. Happy reading.'

We wait for the locked door to click open, then file inside, showing our ID at each checkpoint as we pass through.

As we near the Surf compound, I spot my mother pacing up and down the perimeter fence. Her face lights up when she sees me. 'Anahita, *joon*!'

She hurries towards the gate, her pregnant belly bobbing up and down. Arash looks up from where he's been playing in the red dirt and starts to run towards me too. I show my ID one final time, then I'm in Maman's embrace. Arash's tiny body barrels into my legs, his skinny arms wrapping around my knees.

He squeezes me then sprints off again. He's become obsessed with running; there's so much more space here than on Christmas Island and Nauru.

Maman yells after him. 'Arash! Officer! Officer!'

He screeches to a halt, eyes wide. The officer at the gate isn't even looking in our direction, but it's enough to make Arash sprint back and grab onto Maman's skirt. I hate that she uses it as a threat, but it works.

She looks intently into my face, as if she wants to absorb every thought and feeling I've had in her absence. It's the first time we've been apart since coming to Wickham Point; I wasn't allowed to start school last year while we waited for my immunisation records to come through. They seemed to take forever.

She says, '*Aziz-e delam*, how was it? Were they nice to you?'

'Yes, of course.' I push the image of Jono staring at the bus out of my mind.

Maman eyes my headscarf. 'Did you take that off at school? I told you not to wear it.'

I run my hand over the fabric, feeling the uneven lumps of patchy hair beneath.

'There were other girls wearing headscarves and hijabs, Maman.'

'But not the Australians?'

'It's hard to tell who's who.' I crouch next to Arash to avoid her probing gaze. 'I missed you.'

He copies my words. 'Missed you.'

'I brought you something.'

'*Chi*? What is it?' His face glows with excitement.

I unpack the books from my bulging bag onto the hard earth. I chose the shiniest, newest books from the school library; the opposite of the ones they have in the library in here.

Arash picks up the top one and shoves it into my hands. '*Bekhoon*, Ana! *Bekhoon!*'

I start to read.

KENNY

I see the girl from the bus crouching on the ground near the gate to Surf. I don't want to approach, but protocol demands that I check: what if she's doing something that's not allowed? Has she smuggled something in from school?

I edge closer, trying to stay out of view. There's a book cradled in her palms. Her little brother peers over her shoulder at the pictures as she turns the page. Their pregnant mother shifts heavily, from foot to foot, nearby. The mother is quite striking, really; she's always immaculately made-up, like some kind of movie star. Some of the officers jokingly call her the 'Iranian Catherine Zeta-Jones'. There's an Afghan David Duchovny and a Rohingya John Lennon in here too.

I'm close enough to hear the girl's voice now, reading in a halting but familiar chant: 'Can't go ... over it, can't go ... under it ... have to go ... through it ...'

I think I remember Roxanne reading that story to Lara and Jonathan when they were small. Something about a bear hunt. I never read much with the kids. They teased me about my pronunciation. Still do.

As if she senses my presence, the girl looks up, sees me and smiles.

Cara's words echo in my mind. *They can manipulate you. Manipulate him.*

She has stopped reading now, and waves in my direction, as if beckoning me over. I avert my eyes and walk quickly on, pretending I didn't see.

The soft lilt of her words chases after me. 'Can't go ... over it ... can't go ... under it ...'

JONO

Dad arrives home with an offering of peace:
'Want to have dinner at McDonald's?'
Of course I say yes.
We sit opposite each other
behind a barrier of burgers and coke.
(Now Lara's gone, one Value Box feeds us both.)
Dad asks, 'How was school?'
'Okay.'
I flick the question back at him: 'How was work?'
He says, 'Not bad.'
But his shoulders seem to slump.
He watches, as I take the pickle out of my bun.
I try to sound offhand as I ask,
'What do you do out there, anyway?'
'Security. You know that.'
He inhales soft drink
until slurps rumble in the bottom of his paper cup.
I persist.
'Yeah ... but what do you do, day to day?
I mean, who's out there?
And what's it like?'

KENNY

I cram fries into my mouth, trying to buy myself some time.
In the three months I've been working at Wickham Point,

Jonathan's never asked me about it. Never shown even a hint of interest, let alone come out with a string of questions like this. I shift uneasily, wondering if this is about the girl. Did he meet her today? I want to ask ... but what if he didn't? Maybe – hopefully – he never will. To mention her now might be opening a can of worms.

I decide to tackle the easy question first. 'They're from everywhere. Burma, Afghanistan, Iran. Vietnam. New Zealand too.' I've always found it easier to talk in facts. Emotions are trickier. Messier.

Jonathan frowns. 'I thought everyone out there came by boat.'

'Most did. But some overstayed their visa, or had their residency cancelled. And others just went fishing in the wrong spot. Crossed into Australian waters. They're Vietnamese, mostly. I think they pretty much see it as a holiday from work.'

I'm trying to lighten the mood, but Jonathan is unusually focused. 'So ... why do they have to be locked up?'

The justifications they gave us in our officer training swim readily to my lips. *Defending our borders. National security. Protecting our quality of life*. I'm not even sure I completely believe them, but it's easier to accept what I'm told than start asking questions and risk getting fired. I tell myself I just need to stick to the basics: do my job, get paid, go home and look after Jonathan.

He frowns, as if I'm talking gibberish. 'What does that even mean?'

Irritation swells inside me and I snap: 'Why you ask so many questions?'

He stares at me with his big dark eyes. Those eyes that show every scrap of hurt and pain, and make me worry so much that some nights I can't sleep.

He sits back in his chair and picks up his burger. 'Forget it.'

ANA

We watch *The Voice* on the TV in our room. In the commercial breaks, Maman peppers me with questions about my day. 'What classes did you go to? And what did you learn?'

My answers are stilted and careful; she's got enough to worry about, and I know there are things she wouldn't like. Such as the fact all the classes are a mixture of boys and girls. Or that we're studying evolution in Science; I remember once listening to her debate with Baba about whether it fits with the Qu'ran.

So I avoid mentioning it and describe the grounds instead: the lush green grass, the curving paths, the space.

Arash listens with wide eyes. 'When can I go to school?'

I say, 'Hopefully in two years.'

'I want to go now!'

Maman hugs him. 'What about the Australian students? Were they friendly?' Her voice is tinged with anxiety. Before we came here she thought Australia would make us welcome. But then we arrived to high fences and locked gates. She's convinced it means the Australians don't want us here, and maybe she's right.

Jono's expression flickers into my mind: *Oh, you're one of them*.

I'm grateful when the commercials end and *The Voice* comes back on. Maman returns her attention to the TV; it's her favourite show. We always line up for dinner at the Mess when it opens at six, so we can be back in our room to watch it by seven.

A young black man begins singing a crooning ballad, and Maman watches, almost breathless. He's good. One of the judge's chairs spins to face him.

I try to focus on my homework, using my dictionary to search for words from *The Outsiders*, then look up again as Maman exclaims, 'Yes!'

The final judge's chair turns around.

I grin at her. 'Of course he was going to get through.'

'*Alhamdulillah*.' Maman thanks God for everything, from our boat making it to Australia to contestants doing well on *The Voice*.

A blonde woman comes onstage and starts singing a warbly American pop song.

'Maman, you're better than her,' I say. 'You should enter.'

Maman laughs. 'I could never do that.'

Women aren't allowed to sing in public in Iran. It's been that way since the Islamic Revolution, just a few years after Maman was born. I think about pointing out that we're in Australia now, then realise it's not exactly true; we could still be denied refugee status any day.

Maybe Maman is thinking that too. She says, 'The Husseins were resettled to Sydney. Did you hear that? Meena told me.' Zahra's mother is amazing like that: ask her about anyone and she can tell you if they've been moved, deported or resettled, and the current status of their visa application. She and Maman are close; they have mutual friends in Tehran, which made Zahra and me instant friends as well.

Maman points to a piece of paper beside me on the floor. 'Don't forget to fill out the request form there, okay? Tell them we want to see the case manager. What's his name again? Tom? It's been weeks. I need to ask him about Abdul again.'

I resist the urge to scowl. Abdul is Maman's boyfriend. We've never really got on, despite the fact he's Arash's dad and I adore my little brother. When they diagnosed Maman with pre-eclampsia and transferred us here from Nauru they refused to let Abdul come, because of a criminal charge for punching a wall. If I'm honest, I'm enjoying the break from him, but Maman is desperate to be reunited before the baby's born.

I start to fill out the form. Maman pretends not to watch over my shoulder as I write. The foreign letters and words take shape.

It occurs to me that I could write anything; I could write: *Fatemeh Shirdel requests to go on The Voice* – and she wouldn't know.

The thought makes me smile.

Maman leans forwards, worry in her eyes. 'What are you smiling for?'

'Nothing.' I double-check the form and sign Maman's signature down the bottom.

She reaches around Arash to take it, swatting his grasping hands away. 'Let's hope God turns his chair around for us.'

She laughs, but I can hear the desperation in her tone.

For English, we're in the library again. We traipse down the stairs, emerging from the grey of the stairwell onto the central lawn. For once, it's empty. Quiet. Just a rectangle of green gazing up at the sky.

I close my eyes and inhale the warm, earthy smell of damp grass. It reminds me of hiking with Baba in the mountains in the north of Tehran; we used to go every Friday, me running beside him, two steps for every one of his.

When I open my eyes again the class has moved on.

Zahra calls back, 'You coming?'

But I can taste it now. Freedom.

My eyes fall on a nearby door; it has a sign with the outline of a woman wearing a knee-length dress.

I point to it. 'I'm going to the bathroom.'

'Want me to come?'

I shake my head, but she's already checking with the teacher. 'Ms Vo, can Anahita go to bathroom?'

'Of course.'

I quickly say in Farsi, 'You don't have to wait.'

A frown flickers across her face, but she moves off, following the class.

I push the heavy door open. It bangs closed behind me. I wait for the chatter of my classmates to fade away. Then suddenly it's quiet.

There is no-one with me, next to me, beside me. No officer watching me, monitoring my every move. It's just me. Perfectly alone.

I look at myself in the mirror: it's a real one, made from glass. I take in my wide brown eyes. Headscarf framing my round face. Grin spreading across my lips. I say, 'Ha!' It echoes off the dull concrete walls. 'Ha! Ha! Ha!' The sound bounces and jumps in my ears. I smile broadly at my reflection, splash water on my face, then peer outside.

The quadrangle is silent. Waiting. I step out onto the grass. The sun is hot on my face.

I close my eyes and breathe it all in again. The steamy scent of life. I picture Arash beside me, his face glowing with joy. He never got to go to the mountains in Tehran; Abdul always hated walking, even around the block. He couldn't be more different from Baba.

And suddenly I'm running. I run and run and run for Baba – and for Arash. The warm sticky air hugs my body, and I can hear the flap of my headscarf as it billows out behind me.

JONO

Kicked out.
Again.
Nicked out.
Again.
Gone.
I walk down the snake-gut hallway
to the lawn.
Feel the sun on my skin.

Let it soak in.
Let the frustration
drain out.

'Not listening.
Mucking around.'
'It's called having friends.'
'Don't give me attitude.'
'Everything's an attitude, sir.
Sitting quiet is an attitude.'
'Don't be a smart-arse.'
'Thought that's what we're here for.
To be smart.
To sit on our arses.'
'Please wait outside.'
(Ridiculous that he's polite
even though his eyes are spitting fire.)
But I'm not waiting.
Not today.

Outside it's just me …
and her?
The girl from Science
is running across the fresh clipped grass.
She stops, looks behind,
like someone's following.
No-one's there.
A smile infuses her rosy cheeks.
She runs again.
Almost-skips,

then laughs.
Bell-like, it shatters the silence.
I call, 'Hey!'

ANA

I hear a male voice and freeze.

'Wait!'

There it is again. I turn slowly and ... it's him.

He sees the panic on my face and says, 'Sorry. I didn't mean to scare you.'

My heart is pounding so loud I wonder if he can hear it.

He says, 'You're in my Science class.'

I manage, 'Yes.'

'I'm Jono.'

'Yes ... My name is ... Anahita.'

'You're new here.'

'Yes.' My English vocabulary seems to have shrunk from around five hundred words to one. I think of his expression the day he saw me on the detention centre bus. But I have to ask. I want to know. 'Your name is ... Jonathan?'

His long hair falls forwards, covering half his face, as he nods. 'I like Jono better.' His voice is gentle, almost shy. I notice his hands are shaking. He sees me looking and shoves them deep into his pockets.

I want to tell him about meeting his dad, but while I'm searching for the words, he asks, 'Where are you going?'

I say, 'The library. My class. In there.'

A trickle of sweat slides down my forehead. I quickly wipe it away. Did he see me run? Skip? Laugh? Is he going to tell someone I was here?

He kicks at the dirt, and I notice his worn sneakers say *Dunlop Volley* like the ones I'm wearing from detention. I thought they were clunky and ugly, but if he's wearing them too maybe they're normal here. His have bright yellow laces dotted with miniature kangaroos.

I point nervously to the laces. 'I like ...'

He laughs. 'Really? These?'

'Yes.' That dreaded but safe word again. He doesn't seem to notice it's practically all I've said.

He says, 'My sister sent them to me. She just moved to Sydney. You know the Sydney Harbour Bridge?' A dimple appears in his left cheek. 'What am I talking about? Everyone knows the Bridge. She bought them near there. At some kitschy shop for tourists. You know, as a kind of joke.'

He's losing me. I don't understand. 'A joke?'

He scans my face. 'You really like them, huh?'

I nod, earnest, and he smiles. This smile is wider. Toothier. More real. The dimple appears again, this time deeper. I blush and look away. A small white bird lands on a nearby tree and starts pecking at a bunch of red berries. I stare at it, thinking of the pigeons I used to see racing in Tehran; swooping clouds of feathers dancing in the polluted grey sky.

Jono follows my gaze. He says, 'Torresian pigeon.'

I look at him, confused.

He repeats the words but seems embarrassed. I'm not sure why.

I say, 'Australian bird?'

'Yeah. They come in pairs, I think.' Then, seeing that I don't understand: 'Two, I'm pretty sure there's normally two of them. They don't like being alone ... which means there should be another one not too far away.'

I want to ask how he knows the bird's name, and if all Australian boys know this, and if they ever race them, and if they might be the same as the birds we have in Iran. But as I grasp for the words in English a teacher appears, peering out of a nearby hallway into the bright light of day.

He spots us and calls, 'Jono? You were supposed to wait outside.'

He looks irritated, but Jono doesn't seem to care.

He says, 'This is outside, isn't it, sir?'

The teacher huffs and starts to walk towards us.

I take the chance to slip away.

JONO

Mr Nibbs says, 'What are you doing?'
And then: 'Who was that?'
I say, 'Just a girl going to the library.'
I think: a bird, a stupid bird.
Bet she thinks I'm a nerd.
Of all the things I could say.
Nibbs sighs, 'What's going on?
This behaviour isn't like you.
You're normally okay.'
(Not great, don't get carried away.)

'Are you finding the work too hard?'
I shake my head.
Silence yawns.
He tries the matey approach.
'Everything alright at home?
It's just you and your dad now, right?'
'Yeah.'
'How's Lara liking Sydney?'
'She says it's okay.'
'You could get into Medicine too if you applied yourself.'
'Sure.'
(The only thing I'm sure of is the scepticism in my voice.)
Wings beat the air above us.
A feathered breeze.
A second pigeon lands on the Carpentaria palm.
I smile.
Nibbs watches me, concerned.
'Jono, I hope you know you can talk to me
if something's wrong ...
Or if you want to see the counsellor again.'
I shake my head.
'It's fine. I'm fine.'
And in that moment I believe it too.

ANA

I join the rest of our class in the library, in an alcove littered with beanbags. Jamileh is nestled into one, leafing through a picture book called *The Rabbits*. Zahra is browsing the shelves.

Ms Vo projects her voice so that everyone will hear. 'Remember, it's called a related text for a reason. Whatever you borrow today has to have a link with *The Outsiders*.'

One of the Mohammeds asks, 'What about a movie, Miss? Can it be a movie?'

'I suppose so.'

'What about *Fight Club*, Miss?'

She gives him a wry smile. 'How did I know you were going to choose that?'

The Greek Chorus' ears perk up. 'What's *Fight Club*?'

'It's this movie about guys who fight.'

'And what?'

Mohammed One launches into an enthusiastic description of the fighting and the club and the rules.

Ms Vo picks up a book from the shelf. 'Or what about this? *The Simple Gift*? This is a great book. It's about a boy who runs away from home.'

'Does he fight?'

'Well, no, but –'

'Then I choose *Fight Club*.'

'Me too.'

Ms Vo sighs, then turns to me. 'What about you, Anahita? Anything catch your eye?'

I show her the picture book I'm holding. It's called *Home in the Sky* by Jeannie Baker.

She nods her approval. 'That looks like an excellent choice.'

I examine the cover: a vast blue sky, and a man on a rooftop surrounded by small white birds.

KENNY

I arrive home from work to see my sister, Minh, out the back of our house, spreading compost around some young watermelon plants. She lives not far away in Nightcliff, in a one-bedroom housing commission flat with no garden, so she's taken over ours.

She waves hello, as I climb out of the car.

I call, 'Jonathan home yet?'

She answers in Vietnamese. 'In his room, I think. Dzoung ...' She's never gotten used to calling me Kenny. 'Have you got your roster yet? Can you drive me to the market next week or should I ask Phoung?'

Minh doesn't have a car, just a rattly little motorbike, which clearly can't transport boxes of vegetables.

I sigh. 'It's okay. I can take you.'

I go inside and turn the ceiling fan on to three. It clicks and whirs. I can hear Jonathan's footsteps in his room, but decide to take the rare moment to relax. I pull my damp work shirt off and flop onto the couch. The worn velvet sticks to the sweat on my back. There's a book open on the coffee table. I recognise it immediately: *The Slater Field Guide to Australian Birds*. It used to be a common sight around our house, but I haven't seen it in ages. I thought Roxanne took it with her when she left last year.

I lean forwards and see pencil ticks next to the pictures of birds Roxanne and the kids have seen. Lara's ticks are tiny and neat. Jonathan's are oversized and dark. Roxanne's are loopy and flowing, like her handwriting. Next to a picture of a white bird she's written: *lover birds, always stick together in pairs.*

The words hit me like a punch to the heart.

I close the book and shove it back on the shelf.

ANA

Ms Turner's eyes sparkle at me from the front of the room. She gesticulates wildly, hands flying, as she shows us a map of the world, pointing out all the places Darwin went on his voyage. It's hard to believe anyone would choose to spend so long at sea just to explore and look at animals.

But at least, from the slides, his boat looks sturdy. It is enormous and wooden, with lots of cabins and billowing white sails; more than five times the size of the *Kingfisher*, the boat that brought us here from Indonesia.

Ms Turner pauses mid-speech and walks to the back of the room. She stands in front of Jono and extends an empty palm. He pulls a small white headphone out of his ear, then takes his iPod from his pocket and places it in her hand. It is a well-worn routine; neither of them has to say anything.

I eye the iPod curiously. What does he listen to? What kind of music does he like? And why doesn't he turn it off in class? Doesn't he care that he's wasting a chance to learn? He doesn't even flinch when he gets into trouble; each time Ms Turner raises her voice, my insides leap into my throat.

Not-Jonathan sits beside him; he's not much better. He's constantly distracted by the girl who dresses like a boy. I'm guessing she's his girlfriend, because I've seen them sneak kisses when they think no-one else is watching. No-one else is watching – except sometimes me. And occasionally Jono too. He glances across at them with something like disapproval. Or maybe envy. I don't know.

Ms Turner moves back to the front of the class, and clicks to the next slide. This one is a bird in flight, white feathers splayed against a vibrant blue sky; clearly not Tehran. She tells us that when Darwin got home to England he experimented by breeding pigeons for certain traits, like white or black feathers.

I look from the slide to Jono, and see he's already looking at me.

Something flickers between us, as delicate as a flame cupped in hands, protected from the breeze.

JONO

'For fuck's sake,
ask her to eat with us or I'll do it.'
I pretend not to know who Will's talking about.
Mel rolls her eyes. 'We saw you smiling at her. Again.'
Will's already pushing his way
out the classroom door.
I scramble to catch up,
knocking bodies aside:
'Anahita ...'
(I'm smooth like that. Casual. Cool.)
She turns to face me.
'Hello?'

(It has a question mark, the way she says it.)
Will seems to have disappeared.
I say, 'Jono, remember?'
'Yes.' Her pseudo-bodyguard appears beside her in the hall.
'This my friend Zahra.'
Zahra nods hello.
Will reappears behind them
gesturing wildly for me to continue.
Or else.
I ignore his oversized encouragement,
and launch in:
'Listen,
don't feel like you have to,
but if you want,
you guys,
I mean girls,
could sit with us at lunch
one day.
Just if you want to.'
(What did I tell you? Smooth.)
Zahra angles a protective shoulder in front of her friend.
'We eat upstairs.'
'Oh, okay, cool, no worries then –'
I'm half relieved, but Anahita cuts over me:
'But we can sit with you today?'
I stare. That smile again.
She turns to her friend.
'You'll come, yes?'
Zahra looks me up and down,
like I'm a potential terror suspect,

and mutters to Anahita, 'If you are sure ...'
(Clearly she is not.)
Hope flutters in my stomach,
alongside my nerves.
I say, 'Great, I'll meet you at lunch then.
Next to the canteen.'

ANA

He gives us a small awkward wave, as if his wrist is glued to his chest, then turns and moves off down the corridor. Not-Jonathan runs to catch up with him, laughing and slapping him on the back. I suddenly wonder if this is some kind of joke. *Oh, you're one of them.* My gut twists and turns.

Zahra watches them walk away. Her eyes narrow, perhaps because Jono's shorts are hanging halfway down his legs. He's wearing a belt but that doesn't seem to help; I can see shiny blue boxer shorts and smooth brown flesh.

She looks back at me, incredulous. 'You really want to eat with him? Who is he, anyway? How do you know him?'

'He's ... the son of one of the officers.'

'What? Which one? Tell me it's not Blockhead.'

'It's not Blockhead.'

'*Alhamdulillah.* I thought you'd completely lost your mind.'

'His dad looks like him but ... more Chinese. His name is Kenny.'

'You know you don't have to say yes, don't you? Just because his dad is an officer? It's not like they can punish you if you don't want to eat with their son at school.'

We're walking upstairs now. Up and away from him.

I say, 'I know but ... I want to.'

'Why?'

I can't explain. I don't even understand it myself.

I say, 'Because ... he's different.'

'Yeah, but not necessarily in a good way.'

She's probably picturing Jono's low-hanging shorts.

'Please, Zahra. It's just one lunch.'

'If this was "one lunch" with a boy who wasn't your husband in Iran you'd be rounded up by the police and given lashes.'

'I know. But doesn't that make you want to do it? Because we can?'

I can tell she's wavering, but she says, 'What about after that, if they ask you to eat with them again? You'll think it's rude to say no.'

She's right, but I can't worry about that now. I can barely think beyond today.

I say, 'I might not even be here tomorrow. I could be transferred out tonight to God knows where.'

'Or you could be here for two years like me.'

'Please. I can't go by myself.'

She sighs, giving in, but is emphatic as she repeats my words back to me: 'Okay. But. Just. One. Lunch.'

We meet him at the canteen. He looks up as we approach.

'You came.'

It's hard to tell if he's happy about that or not. I wonder if I've done the right thing by agreeing to come, but it's too late to back out now.

He walks towards the entrance of the school, gesturing for us to follow. Then we're out in the scorching sun, crossing the driveway, angling past parked cars. He sees me hesitate. 'It's cool. We're allowed.'

Zahra shoots me a worried look, but I shrug and wave her on as Jono continues: 'We always sit out here – even when it's raining – 'cause there's shelter. We call it the outer. You know, like, "meet you on the outer". I don't know who started it. Just always been called that.'

He seems nervous, but I don't know why. This is his territory, after all.

We reach a small group of boys, sitting in what looks like an old disused bus stop. It is slightly cooler here, but the air is still sticky and hot. The boys' backpacks are flung around on the ground, and they're talking, eating, playing on their phones.

Jono sits down, leaning his back against the side of the shelter.

I hover, unsure where to sit or what to do. There is not a girl in sight.

Zahra's discomfort radiates from beside me.

I recognise one of the boys from our English class. I remember him saying he's from Sierra Leone, but his name escapes me now. Luckily, he says, 'I'm Ibrahim, yeah?'

I nod hello, but before I can reply he turns back to his phone.

The scruffy brown-haired boy next to him grins up at us.

'Well, hello, ladies ... I'm Mac.'

Not-Jonathan shoves Mac and grins. 'Watch this one. He's trouble. Jono's much nicer.'

Mac shoves him back, laughing. 'Thanks a lot!'

I'm relieved to see the boy-girl appear, in a happy tangle of dark curls. She kicks Jono as she moves past him. 'Bloody Nippy – why do you always get the backrest?' She flops on to the nearby grass beside Not-Jonathan, who is lighting a cigarette.

He flashes us a smile. 'I'm Will, by the way. Take a seat.' His teeth are perfectly white and straight. I could swear Zahra blushes, as we sit down.

The boy-girl nudges him, 'Turn it off, will you?'

'What?' He gives her a look of innocence and laughs. 'Geez. Just being friendly.'

The boy-girl turns back to face us. 'I'm Mel ... Hi, Zahra.'

I double-take, as Zahra says, 'Hi, Mel.' Her voice is stilted and strange.

Mel says to me, 'What's your name?'

My mind goes blank. All I can think of is KIN016.

Zahra comes to my rescue. 'Her name is Anahita.'

Will says, 'Cool. Easy. We can call you Ana. Us Aussies love shortening names.'

Mel says, 'So, Ana ... you from Darwin or didja just move here?' Her accent is so strong it sounds like she's chewing her words.

'Do you speak English?' She speaks more slowly this time, pronouncing each syllable distinctly. In contrast to the fact she seems to be wearing a boy's uniform, her lips are carefully smeared with an almost-translucent pink colour.

I say, 'Yes', at the same time Jono says, 'Mel!'

Her golden brown eyes widen. 'What? It's a fair question!' She articulates slowly again. 'Where are you from?'

I understand this time. I say, 'Iran. Where are *you* from?'

It's a genuine question but for some reason Jono laughs, almost delighted, as if I've said something clever.

He says, 'Yeah, Mel – do you speak English?' His eyes are dancing.

Mel hits him. 'Shut up, fuckwit.'

Zahra flinches beside me.

Will grins. 'I'll give you a hint: her full name's Melita Agape Williams.'

I must look confused because Jono offers, 'Her mum's from Greece.'

Mel kicks him again, harder this time. 'So what? I was born here. I'm a halfie like you, you Nip.'

'Whatever, Malacca.'

They seem to be laughing and fighting at the same time. I have no idea what's going on. I try to catch Zahra's eye, but she's staring at the ground, the trees, anywhere but Mel and Will, who have started to kiss.

Jono pretends to vomit. 'Guys, we've talked about this!'

Will shoves Mel away from him, laughing. 'Sorry! Sorry! Let's eat.'

I try not to stare at all the food: Jono's meat pie dripping with sauce; Mel's juicy red strawberries; and Mac's chips that crunch so loud I hear every bite. Will has a triple-tiered chicken and salad sandwich. Ibrahim's metal containers of rice and curry smell amazing. My mouth waters. It has been so long since I ate home-cooked food.

My face flames with embarrassment as I unpack my pathetic lunch. It's identical to Zahra's: a soggy cheese and lettuce sandwich, an apple and an orange juice.

Mac eyes our meals. 'You guys need to tell whoever packs your lunch to give you an upgrade.'

'They can't.' It's Jono. 'You're from the detention centre, right? I saw you on the bus.'

I'm grateful for the chance to finally explain. I say, 'Yes. I meet your father.'

But instead of smiling, he stares. 'What? What's my dad got to do with anything?'

And suddenly it's there again. That expression. That distaste.

I start to falter. 'I … I meet him … on the bus. He say to … look for you.'

'Ahhh …' Mac grins, like he's suddenly understood a joke. He nudges Jono. 'And you thought she –'

'Shut up!' snaps Jono.

Will laughs, and Mel hits him. 'You shut up too!' she says.

Jono searches out my eyes. 'So you were looking at me in class because of my Dad?'

I give him a hesitant nod. 'He say … look for you … if I need help.'

He winces, as if he's in pain. The smile in his eyes is gone. He scrunches his pie wrapper into a small ball and throws it, hard, at a nearby bin. It bounces off the rim and falls in.

Mac says, 'Slam dunk!' Then there's an awkward silence.

I feel nervous as I ask, 'Something is wrong?'

Mac says, 'Nah, it's nothing, Ana.' But he seems to be smirking.

Jono snatches the cigarette from Will's grasp and sucks in hard, like he wants to inhale the thing whole.

JONO

I drag my feet in the dirt,
as we head back towards the school.
The rubber sole of one of my Volleys
has come loose at the front.
It flaps with every step,
like the tongue of an overexcited dog.
I hear Ana's voice beside me.
'Your ... special shoes.'
I can't bring myself to meet her eyes.
'They're just laces. I can swap 'em over.'
She nods. 'Thank you. For inviting us. For lunch.'
She follows Zahra towards the stairs.
They seem relieved to get away.
Mel punches Will. 'Man, you're an arsehole!'
'Huh?' He looks genuinely bemused.
'Just 'cause Jono's dad said to look out for him,
doesn't mean that's why.'
'Why what?'
'Why she was checking him out in class.
Why she came to lunch.'
'I never said it was!'
'Well, Mac practically did. And you laughed.'
'So? I'm easily amused.

I laugh at knock-knock jokes, for Godsake!'
I can barely look at them.
'I'm gonna head off.'
Will reaches out.
'Wait. Where are you going to go?'
I shrug him off.
Mel says, 'We're coming.'
Her voice is firm.
They trail me out of the school grounds.
As we reach the main road,
Mel slings an arm over my shoulder
and pulls me close.
'Jono, don't get into one of your funks about this.
It's not worth it.'
I say, 'I don't funk.'
But the storm clouds are already gathering around my head.

ANA

Zahra explodes as soon as our feet hit the stairs. 'I can't believe you made us sit there the whole lunch. Do you know how much trouble we could get into if we're caught smoking?'

'But we didn't smoke.'

She barely hears. 'They write it down as a character concern on your visa application. I'm not joking – if you're underage it goes on your file. It happened to a boy just before you came and next thing you know his application for refugee status was denied.'

I feel my blood run cold. I imagine Maman's terror if that happened to us. I say, 'I'm sorry, I didn't know.'

Zahra tugs at the long sleeves she wears under her uniform despite the heat. An ever-present reminder of the scars beneath. A private horror story carved into her skin. She went through hell in Iran, and she and her mother have already been denied refugee status twice.

Guilt overwhelms me. I say, 'We don't have to sit with them ever again.'

'I doubt we'll be invited again anyway.'

She's probably right. The mood changed after I told them we're in detention. I thought Ibrahim might say something supportive, but he was silent. Maybe he doesn't like people who come by boat. In English class one day he said he waited years in a refugee camp in Kenya.

Zahra is ranting now. 'And all the swearing. And did you see those two kissing? Like they thought they were in the movies. And the way they all sat? Legs out. That boy – Mac – even scratched himself ... down there.'

I suppress a smile and ask, 'How did you know that girl? Mel?'

Zahra keeps her eyes on the stairs. 'I had Music with her last year.'

'She remembered your name.'

For a moment, Zahra looks uneasy. But then her usual cheeky, flippant manner returns. 'Well, I am pretty memorable, Anahita.'

JONO

I sink into black,
as we sit in the park
at East Point.
Will pulls out a couple of pre-rolled doobies.
We smoke in silence,
Mel and Will perched
one either side of me.
Like that will make me feel like
I'm not alone.
I think of all the people
– all the women –
in my life
who have left.
Mum, then Priya,
and Lara.
Now Ana's rejection,
another weight on my feet.
Stupid to think ...
Stupid to hope ...
Stupid to say ...
I smoke
until black becomes grey.

KENNY

I stare into the half-empty fridge, trying to construct a meal in my mind. I can hardly think straight with the relentless thrashing of drums from the shed in the backyard. Jonathan is at it in his little sweat box again. His friend Will gave him the drum kit when he got sick of playing it. I wouldn't let him have it in the house, so Jonathan cleared a space in the shed. I thought – no, *hoped* – that he'd soon give up. But drumming seems to be the one thing Jonathan has chosen to stick with.

I pull a carton of eggs from the fridge, and place a frying pan on the stove. A simple dinner.

I wonder if Jonathan has eaten yet, and open the back door. The noise becomes louder; an assault of angry, thudding beats. The last thing I want is another confrontation. But the boy has to eat. He's too skinny as it is.

I approach the shed, reminding myself that I'm a dragon: fiery and strong. But that's part of the problem, really; Jonathan was born in the Year of the Dragon too. We always seem to be clashing over something.

I open the shed door. It slams against the lawnmower, sending bikes clattering against the wall; unused relics of a past long gone. The lawn where the kids used to play totem tennis was dug up to make Minh's garden. One of the bikes is Roxanne's, rusty and cobwebbed. The other two are Lara's and Jonathan's, both too small for them now. I should sell them, really. I could use the extra cash; the latest electricity bill is sitting on the bench inside, and my car rego is almost due.

I wave for attention, but Jonathan either ignores me or doesn't see.

I try again, calling, 'Jonathan! Jonathan!'

The banging finally stops.

'What?' He glares at me.

He's been smoking again. I can see it in his eyes, smell it on his clothes, his hair.

The dragon opens one eye. It's an effort to keep my voice even. 'You want dinner?'

'Nuh.' He starts drumming again. The dragon stands up on his haunches. I reach over and snatch one of his drumsticks out of the air. The wood stings as it slaps my palm.

Jonathan pushes his stool backwards and stands. 'What the fuck, Dad? Why can't you just leave me alone?'

I hold the drumstick tighter. Fury floods my veins. I never talked to my parents like this back in Vietnam. I never would've dared.

Jonathan is ranting now. 'Seriously, stay the fuck out of my life. Why do you always have to interfere?' He pushes his face forwards into mine; it is angry and distorted. 'Did you tell a girl from your work to look for me? Did you?'

My whole body contracts. It's all the confirmation he requires.

'You think I need people like that fucking bothering me at school?'

My mind struggles to catch up. Jonathan must've met the girl from the bus and told her to get lost, probably in worse language than that. I tell myself I should be relieved. It's the best thing that could've happened in a potentially bad situation. A situation I created.

But that attitude.

That language.

The dragon's breath is hot in my ear.

I tell myself to breathe. Just breathe. Stay cool.

I hold the drumstick out towards him, then catch sight of something on the floor. An iPhone, plugged into an extension cord running out the window of the shed.

'What's that?'

He follows my gaze. 'Will loaned it to me.'

Breathe. Just breathe.

I pick up the phone and unplug it. 'No phone means no phone, not that you borrow your friend's.'

Confiscating his phone has been the only discipline technique that's worked. And now it seems I don't even have that.

'Fine then,' he says. 'I'll give it back.'

He holds out his hand, but I shake my head. It's a small victory but I'll take what I can get.

'No. I'll return it myself tomorrow,' I say.

ANA

I sleep fitfully, skimming over dark pools of nightmare, and wake gasping as a crack of lightning seems to explode right next to my head. A rumble of thunder follows quickly after, the sound crashing over me, as powerful as the swell of an enormous wave. It carries me up into the dark then slams me down again. Hard.

The rhythm of panic is loud in my head. My eyes search the dark void around me. I see a glowing exit sign, then another flash momentarily illuminates the space.

I am on my mattress, on the floor, in our room.

The earth beneath me trembles, then there's a sudden onslaught of noise, as if thousands of people are throwing rocks at our roof. Rain. The storms here are violent – everything wild and larger than life.

Frogs join in the cacophony. I'm scared of them; they are so loud. I picture enormous killer frogs waiting in ambush, croaking outside my door, and huddle down into the safety of my blanket, pulling it up around my shoulders.

The fabric feels wet. And then it hits me. The sour, acrid smell.

I realise Arash is whimpering; I didn't even hear him above the roar of rain.

'Ana ... I wet the bed again.'

He was toilet-trained just before we left Iran, but on Christmas Island he started to regress. On Nauru it got even worse. We put him in night nappies now, but they always seem to leak.

I look to Maman, but – somehow, miraculously – she is still asleep. I don't want to wake her, so I push the urine-drenched blanket to one side and stand, lifting Arash up and out of the wet sheets. He latches his small arms around my neck, as another rumble of thunder crashes through our room. I hold him close, feeling the sticky warmth of his little body.

'It's okay, Arash. It's okay. I'll clean you up.'

KENNY

I ring the doorbell and wait, looking around the vast tiled porch. The morning sunlight makes it gleam pearly white. I hear the click of heels approaching the door from inside. Will's mother, Tracy, opens the door, all cream linen and glittering earrings.

'Kenny. Hi. Come in.'

I follow her through the foyer – do houses have foyers? – into the kitchen. The back of the house is a series of sliding doors, facing a pool surrounded by tropical garden and manicured lawn. Inside, it is cool and air-conditioned; I rub sweat from my face, then wipe my hand on my shorts, hoping Tracy doesn't see.

Luckily she's distracted by a fancy silver machine. 'Coffee?'

'No, no. I won't stay. I just wanted to return this.' I place the phone on the marble bench. 'Jonathan borrowed it from Will.'

'You didn't have to bring it yourself.'

'I was hoping we could talk. I wanted to ask ... I think my son is drinking alcohol. Smoking marijuana too. I think he does these things with Will.' I wait for a reaction, but Tracy just nods, so I continue. 'I worry about what it does to their brains. They change, you know? The boys. They change. They've always played soccer, but this year, nothing. Drop out. And now Jonathan, he just sits around. Listening to terrible music. Banging the drums in the shed.'

Tracy looks sympathetic. 'Kenny, our boys, they're growing up. We have to let them experiment. Make their own choices. Even if they do things we don't like.'

'I just worry, you know? Jonathan is … weak. Not like your son.'

She frowns. 'I don't know about *weak* –'

'Last year …' I trail off, unable to find the words. The memory of seeing Jonathan like that still pains me. I've never been good at handling depression; Roxanne suffered from it too. I'm sure it's part of what broke us, my inability to understand. I can barely comprehend the state Jonathan was in last year, even now. All I can do is try to protect him from ever getting that way again. Shield him from potential harm, as best I can.

Tracy says, 'Last year was tough for Jono. With Roxanne leaving, and then the breakup with Priya – he's had a lot to deal with. But that doesn't mean he's not strong.' She hesitates, then adds, 'He's said he doesn't talk to his mum?'

My skin prickles. I'm automatically defensive. 'That's his choice, not mine. She does call him. I can't force him to answer.' I struggle to bring the conversation back on track. 'Tracy … about the drinking and the smoking …'

'Sorry. Yes?'

'I thought maybe could work together. Come up with a plan to get it under control.'

I'm relieved to see her nodding agreement. 'I've already laid down some ground rules. Jono didn't tell you?'

'No.'

'I only let them drink and smoke here, where they're fully supervised. I don't want them out stoned or drunk in the street, mixing with God knows who. And they know if I catch them with anything else, anything harder, there'll be trouble.'

I stare at her, but she seems blind to my incredulity.

'I'm sure it's just a stage they're going through. It'll pass. But, in the meantime, I hope it puts your mind at ease knowing I'm keeping an eye on it,' she says.

I force myself to nod.

ANA

I sit slumped in my chair in the computer lab. I'm so tired that the screen in front of me seems to blur. The teacher's voice drones from the front of the room. Ms Turner isn't here today. Jono and his friends aren't either.

The fill-in teacher has an American drawl to her words. 'Now Ms Turner asked me to get you to look up things about Darwin. So use the internet – but don't waste time. I'm going to be coming around checking you're doing the right thing.'

I feel her pause behind me, so I open the search engine and type in: *Darwin*. A stream of English appears in front of me, screeching down the page.

The door to the computer lab opens and there's Jono. Alone.

Zahra was right: there haven't been any more invitations to lunch. When he sees me, he scowls or looks away.

He mumbles, 'Sorry I'm late. Went to the classroom.'

The American waves him in. 'Take a seat.'

He slinks past her to the closest spare computer, in the corner, next to me. I offer him a small smile, but he doesn't seem to register that I'm here. He chucks his diary and a few pens on to the desk then logs on. Plugs his headphones into the monitor and clicks on the mouse.

Video clips dance onto the screen. I can't help myself. I have to watch. I wonder what kind of music it is and wish I could hear it too.

He catches me looking and glares.

I quickly glance away, but within a minute my gaze has crept back to his screen. The clip ends, and he types in something else. My eyes wander down to his fingers, the keyboard, his pens. His diary. Words cover it like tattoos. Up the top in big red letters someone has written *NIPPY*.

'What are you staring at?' Jono's voice startles me.

I flinch, but force myself to respond. 'What is the meaning?'

'What?'

'Nip-py.' I point to the word.

He's dismissive. 'You know, like, Nip. Japanese.'

'You are Japanese?'

'Nah, they just call me that 'cause of these.' He pulls one of his eyes up at the corner, stretching it into a thin slit. 'My Dad's from Vietnam. You've seen him.' He spits out his words, like they taste sour.

I struggle to understand. 'So you are from Vietnam?'

'No. I've never been.'

There is no warmth in his voice or his eyes. It is nothing like when we talked about birds.

I think the conversation is over, but then he taps at his keyboard, and clicks on another YouTube clip and says, 'This is the only Vietnam I know.'

A picture of a white woman in a shiny kitchen pops up.

I frown, confused.

He says, 'Not this. After the ad.' He holds a headphone out in my direction.

It seems like a small peace offering, so I take it and put it in my ear. We wait and the image changes.

Suddenly we're in a green field with a group of soldiers, guns blazing. A helicopter descends, and Jono nods towards the screen. 'Have you seen this? *Tropic Thunder*. It's fucking hilarious.'

The hack of machine guns is loud in my ears. My body contracts, like it's preparing me to run.

I watch in horror as a solider is shot in the back of the head. Blood spurts upwards like a fountain. Another soldier tries to plug it with his finger, but the blood won't stop, won't stop, won't stop.

And Jono is laughing. Laughing! 'Watch this.'

Blood is everywhere. In their faces. Their mouths. Their eyes. And I'm drowning, gasping for air.

The headphone yanks out of my ear, as I push my chair back and stand up.

The teacher blurs into my line of vision. 'Are you alright?'

But I can hardly see her. The world is a red smash of flesh.

I stumble towards the door.

JONO

The teacher stares at me, accusingly.

'What happened?'

'I don't know.
Should I take her to sick bay?'
'Yes. Please. Just go.'
I hurry into the hall.
'Anahita, are you okay?'
I don't think she hears me.
Her eyes are wild.
Breath shallow in her chest.
I say, 'Maybe you should sit down.'
But she keeps walking.
I call after her. 'Sick bay's right here.'
She finally swings around,
her face a devastation of tears,
eyes jagged black.
I think she's going to yell
or scream
or swear at me.
But she doesn't.
Just pushes past me,
through the sick bay door,
and pulls it shut behind her so it:
Clicks.
Me.
Out.

I tell the teacher she's okay.
But I know she's not.

ANA

I curl into myself on the sick bay bed, as the nurse bustles around me. Memories tumble like an avalanche into my mind. I see myself, younger and smaller, through the haze of years …

… I am standing in the lounge-room doorway,
trying to stay out of sight.

Maman sits on the good couches, opposite an Iranian
police officer. He has a pile of photos in his hands.

'I'm sorry to ask, but if you could just have a look.
We need you to identify him.'

Maman takes the photos, hands trembling, and looks
through them, one by one.

I see a man's body splayed on the side of the road.

A skull of exploded red.

A curve of grey-white bone.

Baba's nose.

Baba's eye …

I feel a hand on my shoulder. The nurse is looking at me with worried eyes. 'I'm here. It's okay. You're alright. Just breathe … that's it … as slowly and deeply as you can.'

She counts my ragged breaths from one to a hundred.

I feel my body start to calm. She calls Lisa down from the IEC. I tell them my stomach hurts. It's true. It hurts all the time; nerves corrode my organs from the inside like acid.

They ask me questions then talk amongst themselves in worried whispers.

I say I just need to lie down. Be still. Rest.

They let me. The room is air-conditioned and quiet. There is no-one playing cards or chess next door, or watching television all night, or arguing through the walls.

I sleep. It is mercifully dreamless.

When I next open my eyes, it's almost time to go home. My schoolbag is on the floor beside me, next to the bed. Someone must have dropped it off. The nurse calls Lisa and she comes downstairs again, and walks me slowly to the bus. Stands protectively beside me. I am grateful she doesn't make me talk.

Zahra arrives with Jamileh. I'm guessing Lisa told them I was sick; they give me small sympathetic smiles.

'Are you feeling better?' asks Zahra.

I nod, still weak. 'Stomach-ache.'

The bus pulls in, and we are counted on. Instead of sitting next to Jamileh, Zahra slides in beside me. She reaches over and squeezes my hand. 'I get stomach-aches too. All the time. Sometimes I think I'm going to throw up.' She leans slightly away from me. 'You're not going to throw up, are you?'

'No.'

'You should drink some water. You look pale.' She unzips

my plain blue Wickham Point–issued schoolbag, and pulls out my drink bottle. Something white falls onto the ground. She bends to pick it up, and hands it to me with a question on her face.

It's a folded piece of A4 paper with *Anaheeta* written on it. There's something inside.

I unwrap it slowly to find a battered iPod with headphones and a carefully handprinted note:

When I feel how you looked,
music is the best medicine.
Jono

Zahra reads over my shoulder. 'What does that mean? Why did he give you that?' I shrug, but she persists. 'I thought you said he wasn't talking to you.'

'He wasn't.'

She frowns and points to the iPod. 'They'll confiscate that, you know.'

My stomach churns but curiosity wins out. I unwind the headphones and hold one earpiece out to Zahra, just as Jono did to me. She shakes her head.

Jamileh's voice pipes up behind us. 'Can I listen?'

Zahra shrugs and turns to stare out the window in silent boycott.

I pass Jamileh an earpiece, then scroll through the list of songs, searching for something I know. I see the name Michael Jackson and press play. And suddenly I'm back in my bedroom in Iran, dancing and laughing and trying to moonwalk with my cousin Yasmin.

Despite herself, Zahra leans in towards me. 'Is that Michael Jackson?'

I pull my earpiece out and hold it between us so she can hear. She presses her cheek to mine. The tiny fountain of music bubbles between us. The song ends, as the city gives way to bush.

It clicks onto a new track and suddenly there is an Australian male yelling in my ear. Every tenth word seems to be 'fuck'.

Zahra screws up her nose. 'What is this?'

Jamileh is laughing. 'Argh! Make it stop!'

I go to press stop, but the familiar beat of hip-hop makes me pause. 'I want to listen.'

Zahra and Jamileh look at me like I'm crazy.

'Are you joking?'

'You don't actually like that, do you?'

I ignore their laughter and say, 'Just a bit more.'

They shake their heads, and Jamileh hands me the other earbud. I push both into my ears and close my eyes.

JONO

I ignore Will's texts
and head straight home.
I watch the *Tropic Thunder* clip again,
searching for clues,
then google *Iran war* on a hunch.
Turns out there was one,

but it ended in 1988,
way before Anahita was born.
I follow the link and read about Iran.
One of the world's oldest civilisations.
Natural supply of gas.
I scan down to 'Contemporary Era'
and skim past the Islamic Revolution
to the Iran–Iraq War
and something about an election.
Nothing of interest there.
So I google *Iran blood* instead.
Images seep onto my screen
of backs covered in whip marks,
and a fountain spurting blood.
A woman's face half obscured by trails of red.
I squirm,
wondering what it means,
and what Anahita's seen.

KENNY

I see Jonathan emerge from his room and feel a spark of hope. For once, he isn't wearing those bloody headphones – that thin white wire running from the buds in his ears to the beats in his pocket. I try not to take it personally, the fact he wears them all the time. The headphones are keeping music in, not shutting me out ... right?

I know they're one of Jonathan's only connections to his

mum; the iPod and headphones were a gift from Roxanne before she left. But it still bothers me to see him like that. Cut off. Plugged in. Wired differently.

He enters the kitchen and heads straight for the fridge.

I have to force myself to bring it up. 'I saw Will's mother today.'

'Uh-huh.' He doesn't even seem to care, just stares distractedly into the void.

I've been thinking about this all afternoon, but I still don't know what to say. Do I try to ground him? Or forbid him from going to Will's? Things were easier when he was little: if I didn't want him to go somewhere I could just carry him to the car. But now he's taller than me. And canny too; he knows that with the hours I keep in this new job he can pretty much do what he likes.

I know Roxanne would call it pathetic parenting. ('You've got to be able to back it up!') But I don't know what else to do, so I say it anyway: 'I don't want you to go there anymore. To his house.'

For a moment I could swear he's about to call my bluff. But then, mercifully, his expression changes and he groans.

'Oh, come on, Dad. He's my best mate.'

'That doesn't mean he's a good one.'

'I've known him since he was five. You have too.'

'His mother said she's been letting you smoke and drink at her house.'

He doesn't meet my eye. Just reaches into the fridge and grabs the loaf of no-name bread, then says, 'What about this? I still get to go over there in the mornings, but in the afternoons I'll come home. That's when they smoke and drink anyway. I won't do that stuff anymore, okay?'

I feel quietly relieved that he's given me a way to maintain a veneer of parental control. For now, at least.

'Okay then. Deal. Sit down. I'll heat you up some pho. Minh made extra today, so she dropped a pot over for us.'

'Nah. Don't want soup. Too hot.' He moves to the cupboard and grabs the jar of peanut butter.

I watch in disgust and disbelief as Jonathan spreads a thick layer then folds the bread in half and stuffs the whole thing in his mouth. I'm about to say something about not wasting Minh's good food, when I hear Jonathan's voice again, part-muffled by the mouthful of sandwich. 'Dad ... do you remember that movie *Tropic Thunder*?'

'What?'

'You got a pirated DVD of it when I was about ten. It's about soldiers during the Vietnam War. Well, kind of. It's funny, you know. Like a spoof?'

I nod, bemused, as I recall: 'Your mother didn't want you to watch it.'

'Yeah, but you let us anyway, one night when she was out.'

A smile passes between us, and I feel myself glow. It's been so long since we had a positive conversation. When I worked in construction I used to knock off in time to pick Jonathan and Lara up from school. We'd sit in the kitchen like this every afternoon, the kids' small legs swinging as they discussed the world and everything in it. Before Roxanne left. Before Jonathan became morose and silent.

He asks, 'Did it ... bother you? Watching a film about the war? I mean, did it remind you about stuff that happened when you were small?'

I blink in disbelief. Is he seriously asking this? Doesn't he know anything?

'I was born in 1976,' I say. 'The war was over. No fighting or explosions. Not like that movie at all. Just sad, poor people struggling. No money, no food.'

'Oh.' He looks almost disappointed.

Maybe I should've talked to him more about how it was for me growing up. Is it too late to tell him now? Will he understand? I'm searching for a place to start, a beginning to the story of my childhood, when Jonathan says, 'So you don't actually know about the war.'

Despite myself, I snap. 'You want to know about the war, you ask Minh.'

He nods and chucks the peanut-smeared knife into the sink with a clatter, then cruises off to his room, closing the door behind him. After a few moments discordant screeches of music scream out, infusing the whole house.

I stand alone in the kitchen, a leaden feeling in my chest, and ladle myself out a single serve of pho.

I put it in the microwave.

Beep.

ANA

Beep.

The metal detector sounds. Milly pulls my bag from the end of the conveyor belt and searches through it. She locates my copy of *The Outsiders* and flips it open to where the iPod is wedged in there with Ponyboy. 'What's this?'

'My friend give it to me. To borrow.'

She raises one bushy blonde eyebrow. 'It will have to go to property to be checked.'

My shoulders slump. 'But … how long does it take?'

'A week. Not more than two.'

'I need to return tomorrow.'

'Sorry. It's got to be searched. Those are the rules.' She says it like she knows it's stupid but can't say that out loud.

I picture Jono's unimpressed expression when I tell him he won't get his music back for weeks.

As if Zahra guesses my thoughts, she leans in and whispers, 'Don't feel too bad. Whatever he did, serves him right.'

Memories bob to the surface, often at night. In one dream, I see myself …

… walking, slowly and silently, around Baba's old study.

I run my fingers over his belongings, like they hold magic I might absorb.

His telescope is angled at the smoggy sky above the apartment building next to ours.

There's a Farad Farzin CD in the stereo.

A Science textbook open on the desk.

A bookmark in the *Shahnameh.*

I flip it open and see the story we'd been reading together before bed ...

When I wake, my pillow is smeared with tears and blood, and strewn with long trailing strands of my hair, yanked out in my sleep.

I inspect the damage in the mirror. More patches of red-raw scalp to hide. I wrap my headscarf firmly, holding it in place with bobby pins.

Maman watches from the bathroom door. 'Ana, I've told you: just tie it in a ponytail, *joon*. Don't wear the headscarf. We came here to get away from all that.'

I pretend not to hear.

She says, 'No-one will notice the patches if you brush it over and tie it tight. Maybe we can ask Meena to find some hairspray for you on the black market to hold it in place.'

I tell her not to worry about it, but leave the headscarf on, as I go to catch the bus.

JONO

She keeps her eyes on the front of the classroom,
away from me.
Her headscarf is wound tight today:
a protective shell.
As the lesson ends,
I make myself approach.
'I, uh ... how are you today?'

She doesn't meet my gaze.
Murmurs, 'I am well, thank you.'
But her voice is heavy,
and the words sound like something
she learnt from a textbook.
Maybe she did.
I ask, 'Did you find my iPod?'
'Yes.'
I try to fill the awkward pause.
'Anything that really got you?'
'*Got me*?'
'Music you liked?'
She hesitates. 'I listen to ... Hilltop Hoods.'
'Really?' I'm stunned.
'Yes. I like. It sound ... ugly.'
I want to laugh, but she looks so fragile I don't dare.
'So, ugly's a good thing?'
She nods. 'Ugly is good ... if it is honest.
If it mean ... you have something to say.
Then it is beautiful ugly.'
I know exactly what she means.
I ask, 'What songs did you listen to?'
'I don't know.' She seems uncomfortable.
I say, 'We could have a look.
Have you got the iPod there?'
She mumbles, 'The officers took it.'
'What do you mean? Will they give it back?'
'In one week. Maybe two.'
'Okay ... Well, when they do ...'
I reach out,

but she reels back,
fear in her eyes.
I say, 'Sorry. Shit. I didn't mean ...
I was just going to write a band name on your arm.
To look up. When you get it back.'
Her arm shakes as she holds it out.
I scrawl letters slowly onto skin
and hope my smile is reassuring.
'This is beautiful ugly music too.'

KENNY

I do an interior perimeter check of the Surf compound, walking slowly along the worn dirt path just inside the internal fence. The mood in the centre seems low today. Subdued. Depressed.

Across the central void, I can see Sand, the compound that contains all the single men. They hang in bored clumps, pacing in the common areas or draping themselves on the fence, staring out. I hate that area the most. That, and the section in Surf for unaccompanied minors: kids with no parents. I hate the areas for different reasons. The kids are an ocean of sorrow; the men are a field of dry grass waiting for someone to light a match.

I can feel their stares following me, even at this distance.

I'm almost relieved when Sally, one of the activities officers, pokes her head out of the computer room and waves me over.

'Kenny! I'm dying for a smoke. Can you keep an eye on things in here?'

'No worries. Of course.'

She gives me a grateful pat on the back as she moves off. I enter the room and automatically count heads. It is unusually empty: just three people on computers. All female. Two Rohingyas ... and the girl from the bus.

'Kenny,' she says.

She remembers my name. It sounds almost foreign the way the syllables form in her mouth. *Keh-nee.* I chose the name when I first arrived here from Vietnam. My new construction mates said Dzoung was too hard to say. Some joked that it sounded like 'dung'. One day, I saw a van passing with *Kenny's Pies* written on the side, and figured it sounded suitably Aussie. But then a few years back a movie came out called *Kenny*; it was about a toilet cleaner, so I ended up having to put up with shit jokes anyway.

The girl seems to be waiting for me to respond.

She says, 'KIN016 – remember? I meet you on the bus, my first day of school.'

'I remember.' I wish I didn't. I'd almost forgotten.

She smiles, like she thinks we're friends. 'I meet your son. He is very nice.'

I can't tell if she's taking the piss or being overly polite. Didn't Jonathan say he told her to get lost? I have a horrible feeling that maybe Cara was right. Maybe by telling her about my son I've crossed an invisible line. The line that says: us here; detainees there. The line that keeps the 'us' safe.

I struggle to keep my voice neutral. 'Thanks.'

She indicates her arm. There's something written on it in pen. 'He tell me about some music.'

I peer closer. The handwriting is sickeningly familiar.

The girl continues, 'Is it alright, maybe, if I can listen here?'

The invisible line rises off the floor and winds around my throat. I sound strangled, as I say, 'Sorry, that's not allowed.'

Her big dark eyes stare back at me. 'I can play it soft. It's for school ... well, a little bit.'

My heart stops in my chest. Is she making a veiled threat, referring to Jonathan like that?

I feel trapped into saying, 'Okay. Just this once. Just quiet.'

She gives me a wide smile then types with one finger, copying the band name from her arm. The YouTube clip loads slowly. Everything is slow in here. Normally I don't care. It doesn't affect me; we have fast broadband at home. But today it is the worst kind of torture, as I wait ... and wait ... Finally, the music starts. It is a song I could swear I've heard pumping out from behind Jonathan's closed door. Angry white men yelling at the world.

My mind runs screaming around the confines of my skull. How is this happening? Did Jonathan lie about this girl? Are they actually friends? And what else don't I know about my son's life?

One of the Rohingya women winces. 'Very bad. Please turn off.'

I lurch towards the girl. 'Yes, sorry. You'll have to –'

She clicks the mouse and the music stops.

Our eyes meet in the silence, and she smiles at me again. 'That's alright. Is enough. Thank you.'

I want to take her thanks and her smiles and grind them into the floor.

JONO

I could swear Dad is watching me
as I lay the table with chopsticks
and a plate of chopped coriander and mint.
(If green had a smell, this would surely be it.)
Aunty Minh deep-fries spring rolls on the stove.
I say, 'Cô Minh ...'
It's one of the only Vietnamese words I know:
Aunty – a term of respect.
'Dad said you might be able to tell me about the war.'
She flashes Dad a look and he shrugs.
'What war?'
'Vietnam, of course.'
'Why you ask that now? It over long time ago.'
I consider telling her about Anahita
and *Tropic Thunder*.
But Dad's eyes are following me like a hawk's,
and I don't want to open up,
just so he can rip me down.
'What year did you come out here again?'
(I add the 'again' because she's probably told me before.)
'1977. I tell you the story already, remember?'
(See?)
'I was in the newspaper.

Picture too.
Me and the others in a little wooden boat,
hands in the air.
So happy to arrive.'
'And then what?'
She sighs. 'You know. It famous story now.'
'Please, Cô Minh.'
I give her my best puppy-dog eyes.

KENNY

I watch my sister and son, the easy banter between them. Minh is getting into the story. She always tells it the same way, even using the same words. She never talks about the journey, only the arrival. I know it was a nightmare trip. Her husband and baby daughter died on the way. I've never pushed her to talk about it, too scared of dredging up tears.

I wonder if Minh thinks I cheated, avoiding the journey, being sponsored out by her so many years later. The baby of the family, the 'lucky accident', always getting the easy ride. But if she resents me, she's never shown it; even when I had the perfect family, all here under one roof, while Minh remained alone. She's never remarried or had male friends, as far as I know.

She gestures with her hands as she speaks in broken English. 'The boat come in to Darwin. Near Nightcliff beach. It early morning. Foggy. All white. Then we see a small little boat. It come towards us, two men dressed in singlet and shorts. White stripes here.' She touches the bridge of her nose. 'Zinc, you know? Sunhat too. And they stand up with beer in their hand and wave. And they come close, very close and very fast to our boat. And one of them hold up his beer and say, 'G'day, mate! Welcome to Australia.' And the people in our boat, they asking, 'What he say? What he say?' She laughs, raw and real.

Jonathan smiles. 'And then what?'

'I stay in hostel in Darwin. St Vincent de Paul give me cooking things, cutlery, pans. I still got them. People give us blanket, clothes, help us find somewhere to live.'

'At Wickham Point?'

She shakes her head. 'There no Wickham Point at this time. Only hostel in Darwin.'

She switches to Vietnamese to ask me when boat people started being detained up here.

I answer in English for Jonathan's benefit. 'There were other centres, but Wickham Point opened in 2011.'

Jonathan ignores me, and keeps talking to Minh. 'You've been out there, haven't you, Cô Minh? To Wickham Point?'

'Yes, I visit friend. They take away they visa.'

'What's it like?'

I feel suddenly panicky, picturing the layers of wire fencing, the endless gates. The sad little rooms and despondent faces.

I don't want Jonathan to think any worse of me than he already does.

I hear myself say, 'It's like a hotel. Bedroom, bathroom, meal area. Normal.'

Minh squints at me like her glasses have gone blurry. She speaks in Vietnamese again and, for once, I'm glad Jonathan can't understand. She says, 'It's not like a hotel.'

'You know what I mean.' I want to change the subject, but she raises a pencilled-on eyebrow.

'Hotels let you eat what you want, when you want. Hotels don't have high fences. And they let you check out.'

Jonathan's eyes dart between us, trying to intuit what we're saying. He takes a random guess. 'Do you carry a gun at work?'

I laugh, as if that's ridiculous. 'No, no, no.'

'But they're locked up, so does that mean you think they're dangerous?'

'Ha!' Minh's exclamation comes out as a high-pitched yelp.

'It's different to when you came, Minh.' I look straight at Jonathan. 'They're Muslims now – like that girl at your school.' I watch for a reaction, but he doesn't even blink, so I continue, 'We might think these people appear nice. They might seem friendly. But they are illegal. Sneaky. After September 11 we have to be careful.'

I picture the girl's overly friendly expression as she pointed to my son's writing on her arm.

I want him to stay away from her.

I want to keep him safe.

I couldn't bear it if he got into trouble. Or fell into depression again. Or worse.

Jonathan frowns. 'Sounds a bit paranoid to me.'

But I'm determined to make sure he understands. 'Please trust me. It's safer to stay away.'

JONO

She appears before me
and presses the iPod into my hand.
'Thank you. For the music.'
I'm caught off guard.
Had almost given up on getting it back.
I manage to mutter:
'Um ... when did you ... I mean ...
When did they ...?'
'They give this morning.'
Despite my musical withdrawal, I stop.
'Did you get a chance to listen?'
'Yes, on the bus to school.
I listen to Hilltop Hoods whole way here.
Only I am listening.
My friends don't like.'
Her smile erases Dad's warning from my mind.
I say, 'I'd bet you'd like Bliss n Esso too.
D'you wanna hear?'
She nods, looking as nervous as I feel.
We hover in the corridor,
a safe in-between space,
that avoids the strangeness
of the outer
or upstairs.
We stand.
And then we sit.
Backs on brick,
side by side.

A thin stream of music
stretched between us,
joining her world to mine.

ANA

We start to sit together at lunch every day. He plays me his music, and I tell him about mine: Iranian rappers like Felakat and Yas and Hichkas. Artists who sing of a future without fear.

Jono downloads the songs for me at his home and brings them in on his iPod.

We sit in an alcove near the stairs, soaking in sound.

I tell him this music is illegal in Iran.

Jono stares at me, disbelieving. 'Are you serious?' Then his face cracks into a grin. 'Actually, maybe we should bring that rule in here. Wish our government would ban some music. Like Taylor Swift. And Miley Cyrus.'

I know he's joking but I can't bring myself to smile. 'No, you would not like. In Iran ... there is no freedom.'

He frowns. 'What do you mean?'

But the question is quickly forgotten, as another song comes on. His body seems to flood with energy, and his face glows, as he says, 'The Living End. These guys were up here last year for Bass in the Grass.'

He tells me it's a concert they hold in Darwin every year. It is out in the open, under the sky, with music so loud you can feel it through the earth. He describes a throbbing, heaving ocean of bodies jumping to the beat as one. Mums and dads trying to look young, dancing alongside teenagers sneaking sips of beer. All together. All free.

I listen in awe, asking more and more questions, stringing my words together in awkward upward inflections.

He laughs, 'What is this – an exam?'

But he seems to enjoy answering. He's good at painting the world with his words. I don't understand all of them but I drink in enough to taste the flavours and swill them around in my mouth.

I ask more. I ask about his family. His life. The words pour out of him as if he hasn't talked in years. He tells me he gets lonely just living with his dad; they barely talk. He misses his sister, who just moved to Sydney and is now living with his mum.

He says, 'It kind of feels like she's gone to the dark side, if you know what I mean.'

I don't. I ask why his mum doesn't live in Darwin.

'She walked out on us. At the start of last year.' His eyes warn me not to ask any more.

He tells me about his house: a small brick cube on a large block of land, empty apart from the careful rows of cucumbers and baby tomatoes out the back. His aunty grows them, and sells them at a local market somewhere called Rapid Creek. He's never been overseas, but he thinks the market feels like what Asia might be like. You can stand there and be surrounded by the chatter of foreign languages, hear the whir of blenders making fresh fruit drinks. See piles of green vegetables and smell the waft of herbs.

His descriptions are so vivid that, for long minutes at a time, they are enough to quench my thirst for the outside world.

Almost.

JONO

We dive down into our own underwater world each lunchtime.

It is quiet and dark down there, just her and me.

The world swims above us in blurry zigzags of light.

We stay below sharing soft-spoken stories and loud-played beats, only resurfacing when the bell goes to signal the end of lunch.

We blink at the bright sunshine as we emerge back into the reality of school.

Will isn't impressed. 'Can't believe you're dumping me for a girl.'

'What are you talking about? I'm at your house all the time.'

I'm there every morning, and still go some days after school despite my deal with Dad. I reckon he knows, but for some reason he hasn't brought it up again. When he's on day shift I make sure I'm home by 6.30pm, and I don't drink or smoke. Much.

But Will isn't satisfied. 'Yeah – only 'cause you can't see Ana before or after school.'

'You're the one who told me to go for it.'

'I know, but you're falling so hard. Getting obsessed.'

'I'm not obsessed.'

'Then why do you have to sit by yourselves? I thought we could hang out as a group, with Ibrahim and Mac, like we used to with Priya.'

But Ana is a world away from Priya. She is something different, amazing and constantly surprising.

And I can't tell him about our private submarine universe – that would only prove his point.

So instead, I say, 'Ana likes to sit in the air-con. You guys could always sit inside with us.'

We both know they won't. The outer gives them the freedom to smoke.

Will shakes his head and sighs. 'Just be careful, okay? I don't want to see you get hurt again.'

I shrug off his concern. 'Who says I'm going to get hurt? We're just listening to music. What's the big deal?'

ANA

Zahra frowns, as I pick up my packed lunch then start towards the stairs. 'Are you going to sit with him again?'

There's no point lying. 'Yes.'

'Are you sure that's a good idea? What would your maman say?'

I pause. 'Are you going to tell her?'

'Are you?'

I've asked myself that same question, lying awake in

bed at night. What would Maman do if she knew I spent my lunches alone with an Australian boy? Baba might not have minded; he was quite liberal. But Maman has always been more protective, anxious, on edge. And she's already so fearful of doing anything that might damage our chances of living in Australia.

'Please don't say anything.'

'Of course. I never would. I'm just worried, Anahita. I don't think you understand ... Australians are different to us. They have different rules. It's like the Socs and the Greasers.'

I roll my eyes. Lately she's become totally obsessed with *The Outsiders*, quoting it and telling me to, 'Stay gold.'

She says, 'Seriously, you can make fun of me, but it's true: it's the Socs and the Greasers ... and I don't have to tell you which ones we are, do I?'

She doesn't. The acid in my stomach burns.

'I just don't see this coming to any good.' My little mother places a gentle hand on my arm. I shake it off. 'This isn't *The Outsiders*, Zahra. No-one is going to die.'

I walk slowly downstairs, trying to pretend I didn't see the hurt in her eyes.

JONO

Dad starts to grumble about his work. His comments seem aimed at me, but I can't be sure.

He's been in the job four months now. Maybe the thrill of being employed again is wearing off.

Or maybe he was always negative about this job, but I didn't pay attention until now.

Until Ana.

Tonight, he says, 'The bloody detainees. They're always wanting things – and the Iranians are the worst. The food's not right. The internet's too slow. They want to see their case manager *now*. Why did they come here in the first place? What did they expect? Rick says they're not refugees at all, just economic migrants who want our jobs. He reckons in their own countries they're all driving around in BMWs.'

He looks at me expectantly, like he's waiting for a reply.

I shift in my seat. 'I don't know if that's true.'

He says, 'That's right. You don't know. You don't know.'

I ask about her past.

First curiously: where in Iran did you live? And with who?

Then guiltily, thinking of Dad's grumbles: what was your house like? Did you have a car?

She tells me that she lived with her family in an apartment near the middle of Tehran. I'd imagined Tehran as a third-world backwater, but from what she says it isn't like that at all. She describes a modern, bustling city with twenty million people and polluted skies from all the traffic. They had a car but just a small one, nothing like the huge four-wheel drives she's seen on the roads here, or the Ferraris the upper classes had in the north of Tehran.

I am almost relieved to hear this. 'So you weren't upper class?'

She shakes her head and explains: those people had lots of money, big houses, luxury cars. They were politicians and government workers. The women draped their headscarves loosely around their heads and wore whatever they liked. The police made different rules for them.

'So were you lower class, then?' I ask.

She wrinkles her nose in distaste. 'No, no. We were middle class. My father was Science teacher – and he work in carpet factory in the night. And my mother was nurse. But we are not – *peinshahr* – lower class.' She says it like it is some kind of insult.

'What does it mean then? To be *peinshahr*?'

'Those people live mostly south of city. They have little money. Old car. They work, maybe like, cleaner or security guard ...'

My face burns: she could be describing me and Dad.

She continues, 'It is very hard for the *peinshahr* to ... keep face. You know? Show good face? This is very important in Iran. To look good ... and be proud. To not have ... old things.'

I ask, 'What was your apartment like? Did you have a TV?'

'Yes, with satellite.'

'And a mobile phone?'

'Of course. My parents have.'

'Laptop? iPad? Internet access?'

She nods.

'But if you had all that, if you were middle class, then why did you come here?'

Her eyes plead for understanding. 'We want democracy ... freedom. We don't want to live under that government.'

I stare. 'But all our prime ministers are dickheads, and I'm not about to jump on a boat.'

'It is different ...'

'How?'

'There ... is ... many ... reason ...'

She's stumbling over her words now, but I persist.

I ask her straight out: 'Why did you leave Iran?

'Please. I don't want talk. I have only bad dream ... Please. Don't ask.'

Her voice is desperate, aching, raw.

ANA

He asks me about my life in Iran, but I can't bring myself to respond. It feels like another world. There is so much that I don't want to think about. So much that I can't say.

I remember ...

> ... crouching in front of the satellite television.
>
> My older cousin, Yasmin, begs to watch an illegal US movie. I tell her to wait.
>
> There is a news item from America about the Green Movement in Iran. Footage from protests across the city in 2009.
>
> I search for Baba's face in the crowd.

Maman moves past, walking her new boyfriend, Abdul, to the door.

I glare, as she kisses him goodbye ...

I feel the sting of hot, angry tears.

Jono reaches out and rests a gentle hand on my shoulder. This time I don't flinch or pull away.

He says, 'Sorry. It's okay. We don't have to talk about it if you don't want.'

Relief pools in my eyes.

JONO

I remember the fear in her face when she watched the clip from *Tropic Thunder*. I remember her staggering out the door. I don't want to be responsible for anything like that again.

So I promise not to ask about her past.

We agree to concentrate on the now. The here. Ana's confidence seems to surge.

In Science, she starts to ask questions when she doesn't understand. I wonder if she realises she's become the teacher's pet, or hears the soft groans each time she raises her hand.

At lunch, I tease her gently.

She says, 'What is a nerd? I never heard.'

'Someone who is ... a bit too smart.'

She beams. 'Really? Thank you.'

I have to laugh. 'Why do you love this stuff so much?'

She tells me about the books her father used to have in his study, about nature and animals and stars. He had a telescope too, and sometimes late at night, he'd scoop her onto his lap and help her look though it, out into the universe beyond.

One day, Turner mentions that the next topic we'll be studying is the Big Bang. Ana thanks her profusely, like she's just been given some kind of gift. Her enthusiasm is contagious.

Later, I ask Ana if, maybe, I could sit with her in class.

She chooses her words carefully. 'I don't think this is good idea. It, maybe, is too' – she thumbs through her well-worn Farsi–English dictionary and finds the word – 'distracting.'

'Distracting, huh?' I grin.

Her cheeks have the faint blush of a ripe mango, as she says, 'Yes.'

ANA

I hear myself humming on the bus. And at school. And in my room. It's been such a long time since I uttered anything but the squeak of words. I'd almost forgotten the way music vibrates my throat awake and makes my head light and breezy. The way it can transport me into another world.

Maman pauses to listen, as we hang up our clothes in the bathroom to dry. It's safer than hanging them outside; no-one can steal them in here. She says, 'What are you humming? Is that something from *The Voice*?'

'No, it's from school.' One of Jono's tamer selections. I feel a pang of guilt.

But then I hear Maman's voice. No, not her voice, her hum. It starts soft, then gradually builds until it erupts in a waterfall of words.

I recognise the song as one she used to sing to me when I was a child.

You are the sky's great moon,
And I'll become a star and go around you.
If you become a star and go around me,
I'll become a cloud and cover your face.
If you become a cloud and cover my face,
I'll become the rain and will rain down …

Arash comes to stand in the doorway and listens in curious wonder; it occurs to me that perhaps he doesn't remember ever hearing Maman sing. The last time she did was at a party with family, just before we left Tehran. Arash would've only been two years old.

Maman keeps singing, and I join in.

I search out her eyes. *Is this okay?*

She's teary, but her heart seems to be smiling as she nods. *Yes, my daughter, yes.*

KENNY

I lie under the car's engine, my back flat on the hard red earth. My dry and cracked bare feet must stick out like a pair of old rabbit's ears, as I stare up into the constellation of mechanical parts above me. Another breakdown. Another budget DIY repair job.

I hear a voice. 'Hey, Dad.'

I almost hit my head. Shuffle my body along and out, and see Jonathan smiling down at me. Actually smiling.

I manage a surprised, 'Hi.'

Jonathan points to our bomb of a red Ford Laser. 'Car gone again?'

'Yeah.'

'You should really get a new one. This is a piece of shit.'

I'm about to launch into my 'money doesn't grow on trees' lecture, but then Jonathan smiles again. So, instead, I say, 'I couldn't do that. You chose this car, remember?' He nods, as I continue, 'I took you out to Palmerston, where they sell the cars on the side of the road. And I wanted the white ute, but you kept telling me red cars go faster.'

'You shouldn't have listened! I was only four.' But there's a gleam of pride in his eyes, like he's still thrilled that I listened to him, even after all these years. 'Remember how spewing Mum was? She kept going on about how she wanted a station wagon.'

I study his animated face in the bright afternoon sun. His iPod is nowhere to be seen. Neither is his phone, even though I gave it back to him weeks ago now. And he's looking at me, really looking, making eye contact and laughing.

I can't recall the last time I saw Jonathan like this. It mustn't be since ... Not since ... Shit.

Not since Priya. Is it possible he's in love again?

My mind flicks to the pretty Iranian girl from the bus, the one with Jonathan's band recommendation on her arm. But even if they have become friends, even if he likes her, they'd only ever see each other in school.

It's not like it could go anywhere ... could it?

JONO

I search Facebook for 'Anahita Shirdel'. My old laptop seems to hum as I wait for the result. Facebook tells me there are eight people with that name, but only one in Australia. There are no photos, so I can't be one hundred per cent sure it's her. The profile picture is a cartoon of a girl with big dark eyes staring out.

I send a friend request with a note: *It's Jono. From school. Is that you?*

I can't help myself. I cyber-snoop and scroll down. I should probably tell her about privacy settings, assuming it's her.

Most of the posts are in Persian script. I click: 'see translation'. But the translator, who calls himself 'Bing', clearly needs more practise. Some things are funny: *I the sea rain fish smile my thanks to my grape.* Others are strange and sad: *What I cry endless air air.*

Further down there are photos, but they're generic, as

if they've just been taken from the internet. A woman in a short dress. A pair of red high heels. A happy couple, arms around each other, walking in autumn light.

There's a link to a website called *My Stealthy Freedom*. When I click on it I see picture after picture of women not wearing headscarves. (Why does Anahita still wear hers? Would she get upset if I asked?)

There are music video clips in Farsi. I watch one by a guy called Farzad Farzin. His voice is deep and crooning. It sounds like a love song. I consider asking Bing to translate the lyrics, then decide not to bother.

I scroll down. There are a few inspirational quotes. Some mention God. (Is she religious? Is everyone in Iran religious? Is that a stupid question?)

Further down still, she's posted an emoji: the outline of a cartoon person weeping tears behind black prison bars.

I didn't know they made emojis like that.

ANA

'You get online much?' asks Jono.

I frown. 'Online?'

He seems suddenly shy and pushes his curtain of hair nervously behind one ear. For once, it stays there; it's growing longer.

He says, 'On the internet, you know? The computer.'

'Oh. Yes. One time every day. Yesterday, I am six to seven. Today, seven to eight.'

He looks incredulous. 'Are you serious? Is that all you're allowed? One hour?'

'Yes.'

'Sounds like some kind of jail ...'

I'm not sure what to say. I ask, 'Your father ... does he tell you? About his work?'

'Nah. We don't talk much at all.'

I've noticed that whenever the topic of his dad comes up the conversation ends in an abrupt full stop. I want to ask him about it, but he hurries on.

'So yesterday you were on at six? And today you'll be on at seven? For an hour?'

I nod, and his brow smooths into something like relief as he says, 'Great.'

I line up outside the computer room at 7.00pm. I think Jono must have sent me something, but I don't know how. He doesn't have my email address, unless he got it from his dad, and that seems unlikely if they hardly ever talk.

The 6.00pm group snakes out past us, and I file inside, showing my ID to the green-shirt as I pass. She records my boat number, and I choose a computer up the back. The green-shirts are less likely to look at your screen that way.

I open my email account. Nothing.

I open Facebook and there it is: *JonoDo has sent you a friend request*. I click accept and his profile fills the screen. There are lots of music video clips, but I don't know the green-shirt and the room is full today, so I don't dare ask to play them.

Instead, I scroll down to see what else Jono has posted. There are hundreds of photos, many of them taken at dark, bustling parties. There are lots of Will and Mel. Mac and a rotating cast of younger-looking girls. Ibrahim and a beautiful African girl who I'm guessing is his girlfriend, because their bodies often appear intertwined.

In lots of the photos Jono looks blurry and wild. There's one of him pulling up Will's shirt to expose his bare hairless chest, pretending to suck on his nipple. Another of him on top of a table with a large bottle of alcohol in his hand. (Did they pay a policeman to guard the door of the party so they wouldn't get caught?) And one of him holding an egg. He looks like he's about to throw it at a passing car, but I don't know why he'd waste an egg like that. We never get eggs in here. Arash asks for them every breakfast.

As I scroll down further, the photos start to feature a girl. She's dark-haired with sparkling eyes and honey-brown skin. She's in almost all the photos now. Laughing. Dancing with girlfriends. In Jono's arms. One photo shows them pressed together, kissing intensely against a wall. I feel like I'm intruding on something private.

I almost jump as a message pops onto the screen. *Hello! 7pm. Your time starts now! ;-)*

I'm glad he can't see me blushing as I scroll back up to the top of his page, away from that photo. Away from the girl.

I type back: *Hello.*

His reply comes quickly. *So … we're officially friends now.*

I type: *Yes.* And then, before I can stop myself: *There are many photos of you on here.*

JONO

I type back: *There's a lot of my music on here too.*

And then it hits me. The photos of Priya. Is that what she's talking about? Shit. Has she seen them? If she looks at my pictures from last year they're kind of hard to miss. I thought about taking them down. I should've taken them down. But I didn't.

I wonder what Ana is thinking now. Did she see the photos of Priya and me kissing, or the selfies of us in my bed? What would she think of that? Ana's told me there was a boy she liked back in Iran, but they were never able to spend any time together. Even if they were just walking in the street they had to be on separate sides of the road in case they were noticed by people she calls the 'moral police'. As opposed to the immoral police, I guess.

I bet she's never even held a boy's hand, let alone kissed or done anything more than that. Mel reckons Muslim girls are really conservative and restrained.

The cursor blinks at me from the computer screen like a frown.

I decide to change the subject and ask: *How come there are no photos of you?*

Another long pause, then her words appear: *You know how I look.*

I write: *You know what I look like too. But I post pictures – most people do.* And then, when nothing comes back, I attempt a lame joke: *You're not one of those girls who hates being in photos, are you?*

No reply. The minutes seem to crawl by. The little green

dot is still next to her name, so I know she's there. But no words appear.

What if she's put off by the photos of Priya? Or doesn't like me anymore? Maybe she thinks I'm a pervert, or an idiot or a jerk. Maybe she doesn't like the guy I am, the guy I've been.

But as I'm spiralling into self-doubt, a new photo appears on my feed. Ana has changed her profile picture to a white guy with oversized glasses and a comb-over, gazing in rapture at a book.

I'm laughing, as I type: *What is that?*

Her message appears: *I google picture of nerd. But they all men.*

KENNY

I hear a gurgle of laughter from inside Jonathan's room. I pause, pressing my ear to the timber veneer. But there's nothing more, just the tap of fingers on keyboard.

I knock, then wait until I hear Jonathan's usual: 'Yeah?'

I open the door and step hesitantly inside.

Despite the open louvred windows, there's an ever-present waft of teenage boy in here. Body odour mingled with sweat-soaked shoes and Lynx deodorant. The floor is barely visible beneath discarded clothes. The walls are covered in posters of bands; I haven't heard of any of them. Where did his musical taste come from? Definitely not from me. I love the crooning harmonies of Vietnamese vocals and keyboard. Jonathan calls it elevator music. His taste is something else. Something angrier, that seemed to arrive with adolescence, like pimples, almost overnight.

'What's up?' asks Jonathan.

I move closer. 'What are you doing?'

I see an exchange on Messenger, along with a picture of a white man wearing glasses. Some kind of scientist maybe. I peer at it more closely. 'What's that? Who are you talking to?'

He angles the laptop away from me.

I brace myself for the possibility that it's a girl. Or, even worse, the Iranian girl from my work.

But to my relief Jonathan says, 'Oh ... just Lara ... sometimes she sends me stupid stuff.'

I realise I've been holding my breath, and exhale. 'Oh ... good ... well, say hello from me.'

JONO

I don't tell Dad about Ana. I've heard all his lectures before.

And, even if I wanted to tell him, I wouldn't know what to say. She's not a girlfriend; the order of things has been completely back to front. When I hooked up with Priya it started as a drunken pash at a party. It was only later that we worked out that we actually had stuff in common. With Ana, I know I like her, and we're friends, but I'm not sure what, if anything, comes next.

Still, I know I'm in trouble when I start to miss her on the weekends.

For the first time in my life, I count down to them with dread rather than anticipation. Two whole days without her curious questions. Two whole days without her cheeky grins.

One Friday lunch, I ask, 'Do they ever let you out?'

She shakes her head. 'Only for school. And excursions.'

I leap at the morsel of hope. 'Excursions? Where do you go? Could I come?'

'Not possible.'

'Or could I visit you one weekend? At Wickham Point?'

'No.' The word bursts out of her like a gunshot, sure and violent.

ANA

I watch as disappointment floods his eyes.

But there's no way I want him to see me in there, like that. Like someone who should be kept out. I remember his expression when he first saw me on the detention centre bus. That stare of sudden realisation that made my face burn with shame. *Oh, you're one of them.* And I remember other things too. The pity in his friends' eyes as they examined my lunch. The way Jono seemed to close up when I told him I knew his dad.

I never want to see that look on his face again. It would break my heart.

So I repeat, 'No', and watch as he folds into himself, hurt scrawled across his features.

'But maybe I can call you.' The words fly out of my mouth and, once they're said, I can't take them back; he's looking at me now with a shimmer of anticipation.

'Yeah? Okay. That'd be cool.' He pulls a pen from the pocket of his shorts, and lifts my arm gently towards him. Writing on my arm has become a ritual between us. An excuse to touch. But instead of a song or band name, today he prints careful numbers on my arm.

'Can you read that?'

I read the numbers back to him aloud.

He nods and says, 'No pressure, okay? I'll just be waiting by the phone.'

It's hard to know if he's joking or not.

It's not until I'm on the bus home that I realise I don't have enough points; it costs twenty to buy a phone card, and Maman already used the last of mine this week to buy shampoo. If I want to call Jono, I'm going to need to earn more.

I'm sitting in the spare seat next to Zahra. Jamileh's sister Shadi had her baby last week; since then, Jamileh hasn't been back to school.

I ask Zahra, 'Want to do an activity tomorrow?'

'Why?' Her voice sounds listless, her usual spark nowhere in sight.

I take in her hunched shoulders. The deep permanent-looking furrow on her brow. The way she's tugging the ends of her long sleeves down, twisting them in her hands.

I remember Maman telling me that, before we arrived at Wickham Point, Zahra had swallowed washing powder when her family's application for refugee status was declined for the second time.

Suddenly I feel terrible that I haven't noticed her slipping until now. I've been so preoccupied with Jono.

I take her hand and squeeze it. 'It might be good for you. We could do exercise.'

She shrugs, but doesn't reply.

I try to wheedle her into it. 'I'll give you my orange rug ...' It's an old one the children's room was throwing out. I rescued it, desperate for a splash of colour in the navy blue and white desert of our rooms. Zahra's had her eye on it for weeks. But today she just sits there, silent.

I make one last attempt. 'And you could use the points to buy a Mars Bar.'

She finally manages a small smile.

I don't let go of her hand.

JONO

I try to keep busy as I wait for Ana's call. I start by downloading music, but Dad soon interrupts. He insists I help in the garden, and I reluctantly comply, hauling oversized bags of horse manure from his car to where Aunty Minh is digging. She always buys in bulk.

She barely nods acknowledgement and, when I'm done, just shoves gardening gloves into my hands, and says,

'Now you do weeds.'

I sigh and pause to check my phone. Again. Still nothing.

I tell myself to relax. It's only Saturday morning. It hasn't even been twenty-four hours.

When I look up, Dad is watching. 'Something wrong with your phone?'

I feel a flare of irritation. 'You mean apart from the fact it's a hundred years old?'

Aunty Minh shakes her head and tuts.

I know I sound like a smart-arse, but I can't help it. I'm too on edge. Why didn't I ask Ana for her number instead of giving her mine?

I weed for about five minutes then check again.

This time, Aunty Minh teases: 'Your phone turn into smartphone yet? Maybe like Cinderella and her pumpkin.'

'You know I could actually buy a smartphone, like a normal person, if Dad would let me get a job.'

'Don't start this again,' says Dad.

'Mel reckons they're hiring at KFC.'

'They're always hiring. Just concentrate on your studies.'

'Can I concentrate on them now then? Instead of doing slave labour out here?'

Dad continues picking tiny red chillies and placing them in sandwich bags. 'Slaves don't get pocket money.'

'Huh. Ten bucks a week.'

'When I was your age –'

'I know. You had no shoes. You only had rice for dinner.'

He scowls. 'It's not a joke.'

My phone's ringtone finally sounds: *Mmm, message from the dark side, there is.* I hurry to get it out. But it's only Will.

Dad's eyes bore into me, as I read the text: *Want to come over?*

I hesitate, but then Dad mutters, 'You're lucky to have a phone at all.'

I throw my gloves to the ground. 'Keep your ten bucks. I'm going for a run.'

KENNY

Frustration coils in my body, as Jonathan disappears into the house.

Minh shakes her head, 'Why do you let him talk to you like that?'

'What am I supposed to do?' I know I sound annoyed, but I'd actually kill to know the answer.

Minh shrugs. 'Use the chopstick.'

I have to laugh. 'Are you joking? Jonathan's taller than me.'

The chopstick is what our dad used on us when we were small. A quick smack on the hand or bum, and obedience was guaranteed. I tried it with Lara once, when she was about three years old, but Roxanne was quick to forbid it: 'That's not how parents do things here.' So instead we talked about 'acceptable behaviour' and gave 'time outs'. And Lara turned out alright, but Jonathan … I can't help but wonder: if I'd used the chopstick on him, back when he was small enough to be scared of it, would I be having these problems now?

The front door of the house slams shut, as he heads out.

Minh asks in Vietnamese, 'What was he saying about KFC?'

'He wants to work there.'

'You mean become a manager?'

'No –'

'Being a manager is quite a good job.'

'He doesn't mean that –'

'It's not as good as engineering, but better than construction.'

I only just manage to stop myself biting back. She's always needling me about dropping out of university for the quick dollars of Darwin's building boom. We end up bickering like an old married couple. Sometimes I feel relief when she leaves and I hear the tinny motor of her scooter driving away. But then I picture her sitting alone, in her tiny apartment with only piles of junk for company, and feel bad.

Minh continues, 'Construction is too unreliable. You injure your back, the work is gone.'

'I don't need it anyway. I've got a new job now.'

Minh just scowls. 'That job is no good. Bad for the soul.'

I sneak a glance at my watch, the red second hand ticking oh-so-slowly around the white face.

ANA

Rivulets of sweat trickle down my neck onto my back. Zahra is on the walking machine next to mine, panting and red-faced despite the air-conditioning. She seems better today, although her long sleeves warn me not to assume anything.

At least she agreed to come to 'Teenage Gym' with me, even though she claims to hate it. The other activities – Computers, Art and the Excursion – were already booked out.

She grimaces, as we chat in Farsi. 'It's crazy that machines like this even exist.'

'What do you mean?'

'A machine to make you walk on the spot? How much must one of these cost to make?'

'Are you volunteering to walk outside in the hot sun?'

'Sure. Just move the big fence and off I'll go.'

I'm relieved to hear her joking again, even if her delivery is deadpan.

She presses a button on her walking machine, slowing the speed while checking the clock. 'Thirty-five minutes to Mars Bar.'

My feet thud on the rubber in time with the pop music blaring from the TV in the corner. American music clips aren't censored in Australia; five girls are jumping around onscreen in clothes that look like underwear. Maybe it is underwear.

'Do you think normal girls in Australia wear things like that?' I ask Zahra.

'Some do. Haven't you seen them changing for gym class at school?'

I have. Frilly matching underwear sets abound. I always feel self-conscious in my worn black bra and thin cotton pants, the same ones we were given when we arrived at Christmas Island. Mine are fraying now, with thin trails of cotton spooling from the edges like spider webs. I put in a request, but they wouldn't give me new ones. 'Still functional,' the officer said. And, looking at the underwear on the women dancing onscreen, maybe they are; there's more material left in them than they're wearing, anyway.

I slow my machine to match Zahra's pace.

The green-shirt calls to us from the back of the room. 'Still half an hour to go if you want the two activity points. Don't slack off now, ladies.'

JONO

I run through the backstreets and arrive at Will's, panting and dripping with sweat.

He's sitting by his pool, already high. He erupts into snorts of laughter at the sight of me. 'What look are you going for there? Sports grunge?'

I got dressed quickly as I was bolting out the door; I'm wearing my old soccer shirt, boardies and a pair of mouldy runners that are at least a size too small. I tell him to shut up, as I take a seat by the glistening pool. I'm tempted to jump in, but settle for splashing my face with water. It's as warm as a bath.

'I can't stay long. Told Dad I was going for a run.'

'Well, that'd buy you a few hours, wouldn't it? You're pretty slow.'

'Piss off.' I check my phone again. Still nothing from Ana.

'Where's Mel?' I ask.

'At work. She said to find out if you wanted to apply.'

'I can't.'

'Your dad?'

'Got into another fight with him about it this morning.'

'Did he see you in that povo outfit? That might've convinced him you need the cash.'

I know he's joking, but the remark stings. I look at Will lounging back in his deckchair: his new boardies, designer sunnies, label T-shirt, easy grin. It's not that I'm jealous of him – I've never had to be, because he shares. His whole family is incredibly generous. Tracy feeds me almost every morning, and Will's dad, Tony, often shouts us movies and pizza. They're always saying their house is my house. Except I know it's not.

Will picks a pre-rolled doobie out of a bowl on the ground beside him. 'Here's a little something I prepared earlier.'

He lights up, takes a few lazy drags then passes it to me. 'It's been seriously good stuff lately. I've bought extra the last few times.' He tosses a small sandwich bag holding fat heads of pot into my lap. 'You can have that if you want.'

I don't argue; my personal stash is running low. I stuff it in my pocket. 'Thanks ... Where'd you get the cash from?'

'Saved up my pocket money.' He gives me a wink. 'It's cheaper anyway. To buy a whole lot at once.'

'In bulk?' I ask.

He nods. 'Better for resale too.'

My brain hurries to catch up. 'So what – you're selling now?'

'Just a bit here and there.'

'But ... why? It's not like you need the money.'

'It's fun.' He gives me a lazy shrug. 'And I can buy extra stuff. Like these sunnies.'

'Yeah?' A spark of possibility ignites in my brain. 'What kind of profit do you make?'

Will pulls out his phone and walks me through the numbers. I've never seen him do maths so fast, apart from calculating the odds in sport.

My eyes widen at the final figure on his screen. 'Shit. That's not bad.'

'You want to help?'

'I think, maybe, I do ... just sometimes ... yeah ...'

Will grins. 'Cool.'

ANA

We wait in the queue for the shop. When we finally get to the front, Zahra tells the officer her boat number then mine.

'Two Mars Bars, please.'

I jump in quickly. 'Sorry – one only.'

She frowns. 'That *one* better be for me.'

'It is.'

The officer gets a half-melted chocolate bar from the back of the shop and shoves it towards Zahra. 'Next!'

I hurry to blurt it out: 'One phone card, please.'

'Sorry, sold out. Try tomorrow. Next!' We're bustled out of the way, as the people behind us push forwards.

Zahra narrows her eyes. 'What's the phone card for? You're not calling *him*, are you?' My blush confirms it, and she shakes her head. 'You're crazy.'

'I'm not doing anything wrong.'

'I don't get it. Why do you like him so much?'

I struggle to put it into words. 'He ... treats me like ... a normal person. An Australian.'

She almost laughs. 'But you're not. Do you think Australians live like this? We're the lowest of the low here. Worse than *peinshahr*.'

Her words cut close to the truth, but I say, 'That's nothing to do with Jono.'

'His dad's an officer.'

'One of the good ones – you said so yourself. And Jono's good too.'

'He's a Soc.'

'You don't even know him, Zahra. If anything, he's more like Ponyboy. He's sensitive and smart. And I don't think his dad's rich at all.'

'Yeah, but he's got privileges. Freedom. Rights. He might have worries, but I bet he's never been scared for his life. Which means he's a Soc. He'll never understand what it's like to be us.'

Ever since I arrived, Zahra's been the authority, the one who's been here longer and knows more. But this time I challenge her. 'How do you know? You're not even friends with any Australians.' Zahra hardly mixes with the mainstream kids. She holds herself apart.

She hesitates, then says, 'Remember, I had Music with Mel last year.'

It takes me a moment to work out who she's talking about. 'Jono's friend?'

She nods. 'We used to sit together in class. Then the school held a Year 9 dance and I was so excited – they were going to let us out for it – but I didn't have anything to wear. The officers wouldn't help, and I didn't have money to buy something on the black market. So I made the mistake of asking my Australian 'friend', Mel, if she owned any dresses. It was like lighting a match. She was furious. She thought I was making fun of her dressing like a boy. And my English wasn't good enough. Before I could explain, all this hatred came pouring out. She said at least she had a mind of her own, unlike Muslim women, who are so oppressed that even the boat people pluck their eyebrows.' Her voice is shot through with pain. 'She couldn't see ... or listen ... or understand ... that this' – she gestures towards her immaculate eyebrows – 'is a small freedom. One little thing I can control. That I choose this the same way she chooses shorts over skirts.'

I ache for her. I ache for me.

'What about the formal?'

'I didn't go. The only clothes I had were the ones they give us in here. I couldn't show up like that. I wanted to feel like a normal teenager ... even if just for one night.'

Her words feel like an echo of my heart.

I remember ...

... kissing Maman goodbye, as Yasmin and I head out the door.

Abdul stands behind her, holding my new baby brother, Arash.

It is a relief to pull the door closed behind us as we go.

Outside, the air is warm and sticky. Yasmin grins, conspiratorially. 'Are you wearing something different under that?'

I am.

She takes me to her friend's apartment, my first underground concert. We shed our hijabs and a layer of clothes at the door.

Yasmin gives my singlet top and short skirt an approving nod. The room is pulsing with bodies and beats. We push through them towards the makeshift stage. There's a woman rapping about the oppression of forced marriage.

I stand still, listening with an open mouth.

Yasmin tugs at my hand and we start to move, laugh, dance.

I feel completely alive ...

I look back at Zahra, and take her hand. 'I'm sorry that happened with Mel. And I'm sorry you couldn't go.'

Her eyes are watery, but she forces a smile. 'Maybe this year.'

'For sure.' I want to entertain her dream. 'What do you think it feels like? That kind of freedom?'

She thinks for a moment, then says, 'I think it feels like ... jumping into a clear pool of water. Or falling through a star-filled sky.'

JONO

I run home through a monsoonal downpour of rain. It strips the humidity from the air. The earth smells steamy and rich. My mouldy runners slap through puddles, sending up showers of muddy spray. My clothes and hair are soaking, but I don't care. Will's sandwich bag of pot is safe and dry in my pocket.

I've been out ages; Dad has texted more than once. I messaged back that it had started raining and I'd stopped in at Nightcliff Library to read. I've learnt that half-truths are more likely to be believed than complete lies.

The rain eases, as I run across Trower Road, dodging the cars.

I stop and check my phone for the hundredth time today. Still no call from Ana. But in my stoned state even the thought of her makes me smile.

I jog the last block home, as the sky erupts in a riot of pinks and reds.

ANA

The clouds are on fire, and there's a pale crescent of moon. I stare up at it from the Wickham Point playground, as Arash does laps of the slide. He clambers up the steps and swooshes down the smooth blue plastic, before running back around and doing it all over again.

Zahra and Jamileh sit talking on a bench nearby. Jamileh

has her sister Shadi's baby cradled in her arms. 'He sleeps so much during the day, but at night ...' Her words are slow and deliberate, as if even the effort of stringing them together is almost too much.

'Do you think you'll be able to come back to school?' asks Zahra.

'I don't know. I want to but ...' Jamileh trails off.

I know the 'buts'; I'm all too aware her situation could soon be mine.

Zahra catches my worried frown and says, 'Don't worry, Ana. I already heard my mum telling your mum she'll help when the baby comes.'

We're distracted by an argument erupting near the swings. Some little kids face off against each other, one versus two.

'Are you playing or not?' The 'one' has her hands on her bony little hips. She couldn't be more than eight. 'If you want to play you have to look sad. You're the detainees. We're the officers. If you don't look sad we'll send you to Nauru.'

The other two decide they'd better comply. They sit huddled together on the fake grass and pretend to cry, while the boss-girl marches around them yelling orders.

When I look back at Jamileh, there are tears trickling down her cheeks. 'I'm scared they'll send us back there now the baby's born. I've heard people talking ... that pregnant woman upstairs from us even tried to kill herself last night ...'

Zahra says, 'I hate seeing babies in here, let alone thinking about what it must be like for them on Nauru.' There is a hardness to her voice I haven't heard before. But she doesn't say anything to try to ease Jamileh's fears; the reality is that none of us know where we'll be tomorrow, let alone next month.

An Afghani woman appears and calls the children back to their rooms. All three of them disappear.

Jamileh stands. 'I should get back too.'

'I'll come,' says Zahra.

The light is fading fast; I slap at the midges biting my arms and legs. 'Arash,' I call. 'Can we go?'

'One more, Anahita. One more.'

My friends give me amused and sympathetic looks as they leave.

We are alone now, just me and Arash. In the distance, I see dark specks of birds flying home for the night. I make my eyes go blurry so the fences dissolve into dusk. It is almost beautiful. I take a deep breath in.

When I focus my eyes again, the birds are overhead. Their silhouettes are ragged, like pieces of dark cloth fluttering in the sky. They are noisy, screeching, raucous. They are not birds at all. They're bats.

A shiver runs down my spine, as if a cold breeze has blown into my body and out the other side.

In a flash, I see myself ...

... walking along the street in the grey light of afternoon.

Omid, a boy I like from school, keeps pace with me on the footpath on the other side of the road.

We smile at each other over the passing cars.

I look up, and see racing pigeons wheeling through the pale brown sky.

Something pointed and metal presses into my back.

Omid's expression has changed. He looks fearful.

I know that it is a gun ...

My whole body is shaking as I hurry to the slide. 'We have to get back, Arash. It's time to go inside.'

He takes hold of my hand, as we walk back towards the rooms.

I hear his small voice: 'When are we going to Australia, Ana?'

I squeeze his fingers gently. 'Soon, Arash. Soon.'

JONO

I wake to the feel of light cotton sheets soft on my legs. The warm air from the fan caresses me from above. I hear the chirping of cicadas outside and slowly open my eyes.

I'm in my room. My phone is on the bedside drawers. And it's ringing. Shit, it's ringing. I snatch it up.

No Caller ID.

'Hello?'

Her voice swells to fill the line. 'Jono? Is that you? I wake you up?'

'No ... no. It's fine. How are you?'

There's a pause, then I can hear a grin in her voice, as she says, 'Do you want Australian answer?'

'Go on then.'

'Good.'

'Is that it?' I laugh, and she laughs too.

'Yes. That is it.'

'So what's the Iranian answer then?'

I wander out to the lounge room as we talk. I want to make sure Dad's not home; he usually leaves early on Sundays to help Aunty Minh at the market. I'm glad to find the house empty and quiet. I flop onto the lounge in my boxer shorts.

'In Farsi we ask: *Haal-e shomaa chetoreh*? It is the same: how are you? But when I answer, when I am little, my father never let me say good or okay. Because he says he is asking about the feeling, you know … like, how is your heart?'

I smile, feeling high on the sound of her voice.

'My heart is happy,' I say. 'Happy you called.'

ANA

Courage seems to come easier on the phone. I ask him things I've wanted to know but haven't dared to ask. Like why he always seems tense when he talks about his dad.

He says, 'We used to be close. But when Mum left things changed. He was really bitter, only ever mentioned her to snipe or put her down. He made me feel like I had to choose. So I chose him, of course. He was the parent who'd stayed. My sister, Lara, lives with my mum now – she moved for uni.'

I ask, 'Why your mother … leave?'

'She wanted to *find herself*.'

I have no idea what that means. What part of herself couldn't she find at home, in the safety of Darwin, with her whole family around her? I say, 'I don't understand.'

'Yeah. Me neither.' His voice breaks slightly.

'But you do not talk to her? Now?'

'She calls sometimes, but I don't pick up.'

That makes a strange kind of sense to me. We don't call our family in Iran anymore either. We did at first, but every time we spoke to them they were expecting good news. It was too hard to keep breaking their hearts and ours.

I say, 'Because it is pain?'

'Exactly.' He sounds relieved I understand.

I ask about the girl in the photos. It's been bugging me ever since I saw them. Who was she? And what did she mean to him?

He tells me her name is Priya.

'She was your girlfriend?'

'Yes.'

'You did love her?'

There's a pause. He says, 'I thought I did … but maybe it was something else. After Mum left I was really down. I never wanted to go home. Lara was busy studying for Year 12, and Dad was grumpy as hell. Then Will and Mel hooked up, and suddenly there was Priya. I needed her. She saved me, really. I practically lived at her house.'

It's strange to hear about him so wrapped up in another

girl's life. Jealousy sears me from the inside at the easy way he describes their lives fitting together. What would it be like to live alongside Jono every day? To be an 'us'? To have our lives enmeshed, intertwined, shared?

JONO

Ana is even more direct and curious on the phone than she is face to face. She asks about Priya, and I'm surprised to find that it doesn't hurt to talk about her as much as it once did. I tell her about Priya's parents deciding to move to Perth, and how she broke up with me weeks before she left. I'd wanted to try long distance, but she refused. Said she didn't love me anymore, that she thought of me more as a friend.

I say, 'I don't like talking about it much.' I borrow Ana's words: 'Because it is pain ... I guess.'

I hear her say, 'Yes.'

About a month after Priya left she texted from Perth to say she'd met someone else. I tried to call her after that, but she wouldn't even answer the phone.

I was so low I couldn't get out of bed for days, maybe weeks. I just listened to 'beautiful ugly' music and cried. In class. Over dinner. At soccer. At home. It poured out of me, uncontrollable, until Dad snapped, yelling at me to stop being so pathetic and weak.

'Path-e-tic?' says Ana.

I want her to understand. I need her to understand.

'I was just so down, you know? I was at zero.' A term the school counsellor used at the time. It doesn't help to clarify the situation now.

'What does that mean? Zero?' asks Ana.

I search for another way to say it. A way that's mine. 'It's when you're so far down you can't see the light above.'

There's a horrible silence on the line.

I say, 'Ana? Are you there?'

If she too thinks I'm pathetic and weak I will die.

But then I hear her voice, soft and wavering through the phone. 'Yes. I know this place with no light. But I don't think you are weak. I think you are brave. You wear your feelings ... outside. I do not.'

Relief and gratitude rush through me. 'You can if you want. I mean, you can with me. I hope you know that.'

She says, 'Thank you', but doesn't say anything more.

ANA

Memories flood my body, so fast and deep that I might drown. I see myself ...

> ... being herded into a crowded minibus, by the morality policeman and his gun.
>
> He grabs me and shoves me forwards, yelling for me to 'Get the fuck on!'

Inside, one woman is wearing red lipstick, another puffs openly on a cigarette.

They drive us to the central part of Tehran.

The policemen shout at us: 'You sluts!'

'Why are you wearing lipstick?'

'Have you been sleeping with a man?'

Hours later, I stand in front of a judge and a priest and tell them I've done nothing wrong. I'm not wearing any makeup or showing my hair. My *mantoue* is the right length.

Omid isn't there; he must've got away.

The policemen let me go, pushing me out the back door into an empty street.

It is 1.00am. I am completely alone.

A man in a silver car pulls up beside me and asks how much for an hour in a hotel.

I see a parked taxi up the road and run towards it as fast as I can.

The driver wakes up and, luckily, is kind enough to drive me home.

Maman weeps in relief, and thanks him over and over again, as she pays the fare …

My mouth is open. I want to tell Jono but nothing comes out. I remember Zahra's words. *They don't know what it's like to be scared for their life. They will never understand what it's like to be us.*

I tell myself that if anyone might understand, it would be this boy who wears his emotions like clothes, on the outside, for everyone to see.

But I am not like that.

I can't afford to be.

So I stay quiet.

KENNY

I watch for changes in Jono's mood, just like the counsellor last year advised. But to my relief, he seems happy lately. Content. When he helps in the garden on Saturdays, he doesn't complain as much as he used to. Sometimes he even whistles upbeat tunes as he works, melodies that I don't recognise or know.

His phone seems to ring more often. He disappears into his room to talk, sometimes for up to an hour. I ask who's calling, but he just looks cagey and answers with that frustratingly all-encompassing Aussie term: 'Mates.'

I phone Lara for one of our regular chats. I hope I don't sound tense, as I ask, 'Are you at your mother's?'

'No, I'm at uni, studying ...'

I relax slightly in the knowledge that she isn't at home with Roxanne.

Lara continues, 'But I can talk. What's up?'

I love hearing her open, friendly voice. I miss her every day. As much as I'd love to know, I never ask how she finds living with her mother. Instead, I ask about Medicine, and if she likes being in Sydney, and if the weather down there is cold.

Today I add an extra question to the list: 'Do you know ... does Jonathan have a girlfriend?'

'Not that I know of – but we haven't talked in ages.'

Alarm bells sound in my mind. 'I thought you two chatted on Messenger quite a bit? And don't you call him?'

Lara sounds suddenly guilty. 'I've been busy, Dad. Medicine isn't like high school.'

'Of course.'

When I hang up, I have a queasy feeling in my gut.

If he hasn't been talking to Lara, then who's been calling him on the phone?

ANA

'Where have you been?' Maman looks up from her mattress on the floor, as I enter the room.

'Talking ... to a friend.' I don't tell her the friend's name or say it was on the phone. I call Jono quite often now – mostly on the weekends, but sometimes after school. When my scheduled hour suits, I phone during my computer time so Maman doesn't find out. Other days I lie and tell her I'm going to study with Zahra.

Today, she is too preoccupied to ask any more. 'You missed dinner. I had to take Arash. Which was lucky because we got this.' She waves a visit slip in my direction. 'Tom, our case manager, is finally coming. Tomorrow at 3.30pm. You'll have to skip school.'

'No.' The word shoots out of me before I even realise it is there. 'I'll be back in time. The bus gets in at three twenty-five.'

But Maman shakes her head. 'We can't risk it.'

I always go to appointments with her: the doctor, the counsellor, the lawyer, Tom. She's terrified she won't understand something important if I'm not there. Most times they provide an interpreter but sometimes they're just on speaker phone, not even in the room. And, anyway, Maman doesn't trust them like she trusts me.

I say, 'Maman, I'll be here. I promise. Please can I go?'

She studies me with a glow of pride. 'It's important to you. This school.'

I nod, guiltily. School is important. But something else is too.

At lunchtime Jono says, 'Hey, I was thinking, we should video call some time. On Facetime or Skype ... do you have either of those on the computers?'

I hesitate. It's not that we don't have the programs or aren't allowed; Maman uses Skype to talk to Abdul every other day. But if I start calling Jono from the computer room, someone is bound to notice and tell Maman. The room is always full.

So I say, 'It is the same as we talk on the phone.'

'Sure ... but this way I could see your face.' I catch the hint of a blush beneath his tanned skin.

I'm touched, but there's no way I can agree. 'The cameras are not on ... on the computers.'

'I can tell you how to fix that –'

'No! I mean, we are not allowed. The cameras are not allowed.'

'But why not?'

'Same reason as we are not allowed to put photos on Facebook. Zahra says ... they don't want people to know ... to know us ... to know we are here.'

He looks at me, and it is like he sees straight into my soul. 'Well, they failed. 'Cause I know you.'

I am in a basement in central Tehran, with my whole body pressed up against Omid. Our lips mash together, and my heart races as his hands explore. I feel them over my belly, my breasts, my nipples, my bum. Around us, people are dancing, talking, kissing, laughing, singing.

The rapper up the front yells for us to all join in for the chorus. We all scream the words together; they are lyrics mocking a famous Imam. The chant turns to shouts and screams midway through.

The morality police pluck people from the crowd, lining the boys up on one side of the room, and the girls on the other.

They smell our breath for alcohol, one by one.
Omid is taken before me.

This time, the judge and priest don't send me home.

I feel the the whip cut into the flesh on my back,
again and again and again and again …

I jump, as Jono touches my arm.

'What are you thinking about? Sometimes you get this look. It makes me nervous.'

There is concern in his eyes, but I pull back. Away.

'Nothing,' I say. 'It is nothing.'

KENNY

I see the girl's mother scolding her, as they hurry down the path. The little brother sprints ahead. The girl practically has to skip to keep up. As they near the meeting room, a young blonde woman peers out the door. I haven't seen her before, but she has a pass around her neck. A new case manager. They're getting younger all the time. This one couldn't be long out of university.

I feel the familiar sting of regret. I'd never admit it to Minh but sometimes I wish I hadn't dropped out. If I'd stuck at it, where would I be now? I know one thing: I wouldn't be here.

I startle as I hear a voice behind me.

'Afghan Catherine Zeta-Jones. She's a looker, huh?' I turn to see Rick grinning.

When I look back, the mother and boy have disappeared into the room. The girl pauses to close the door behind them, and catches sight of me across the yard. Her face lights up and she waves. The gesture is both pleased and familiar. I cringe.

Rick frowns. 'Wait – the daughter? You serious? You better be careful there. She's pretty, okay? But she's what – sixteen? Seventeen? Illegal in more ways than one.'

'It's not like that –'

'Sure, sure.'

'It's not.'

He shrugs. 'Fine. But whatever you do, don't give 'em special treatment or you're screwed. Like Fiona – you know why she got fired? She was giving out extra … what do you call 'em? You know, women's stuff. Sanitary napkins – handing them out left, right and centre. Detainees found out she was a soft touch, of course. They were probably just bunging it on, asking for extras to sell on the black market. And she was sacked over it.'

His story makes me squirm. There's no way I can afford to lose this job.

'I don't even know that girl,' I say. 'Maybe she thought I was someone else.'

But it sounds unconvincing, even to me.

ANA

Maman stares at the young blonde woman sitting across the desk, then asks in Farsi, 'Who is that?'

The question is directed at me, but the interpreter jumps in. Her name is Habibeh; we've had her before. She says, 'This is Eliza Moore. She's a new case manager.'

Eliza extends a hand.

Maman shakes it warily, and asks, 'Where is Tom?'

Eliza gives us a small nervous smile. 'Oh, sorry. Tom's on long service leave. They didn't tell you?'

'No.' Maman scratches at the red polish on her nails, a sure sign she's nervous. I understand her concern. Eliza is the third case manager we've had since arriving at Wickham Point, and can't be more than five years older than me. She is slender, with short-cropped hair and an easy smile.

She says, 'I'm picking up a lot of Tom's cases. I just started work for the Department. I'm from Melbourne originally. Not used to this heat.' She laughs nervously and hurries on. 'But I'm happy to be here, and it's great to meet you, Fatemeh ... and Anahita ... and you must be Arash.' She smiles at him, and Arash climbs eagerly from my lap to hers. She laughs again. 'Oh, hello! You're very friendly, aren't you?' She unwraps his little arms from around her neck and props him on one knee. 'You can stay there if you want, but I'm going to talk to your mum, okay?' She jiggles him up and down. He giggles happily and Eliza beams at me and Maman. 'Now, tell me. How have you been feeling lately?'

Habibeh finishes translating, and there's a deafening

silence. I can guess what Maman's thinking: what does this new woman mean for our case? And what happened to the application we lodged with Tom to get Abdul here from Nauru?

Eliza consults the page in front of her. 'Let's see: medical issues. How are they going at the moment? I mean, Fatemeh, you're pregnant, obviously ... are you feeling okay? This says you were transferred here with pre-eclampsia. High blood pressure. Have you seen your doctor lately?'

I answer for Maman. 'Last Wednesday.'

'Great. And what about your lawyer?'

'We have a letter, but they are in Sydney and cannot come.'

Maman erupts in a stream of Farsi. 'My boyfriend, Abdul, is on Nauru. He's the baby's father. I need him here. We lodged so many requests with Tom. And this baby is due in just a few weeks. I need Abdul here for the birth. Please. I can't, I won't have the baby if he's not here.'

It is devastating to hear her empty threats and desperate pleas. She's been strong for me and Arash. But now her fear rains down on us, like a Darwin storm, ferocious and wild.

Eliza listens to the translation. Her eyes fill with tears. I can't help but stare; none of our other case managers have shown much emotion at all. She dabs at her eyes, then looks through the papers in front of her yet again. 'I can see here you have an application in for family reunion. That's a start and, even with the criminal charge against him, I'd say you have a good case with the baby due so soon. I'll try to escalate it, okay?'

Maman clings to this drop of hope, so grateful she begins to weep.

The sound of her sobs makes my chest contract.

I see myself …

… sitting in a lukewarm bath, knees tucked into my chest.

The water around me is tinged with blood, and the cuts on my back sting.

I can hear Maman and Abdul arguing down the hall.

Maman is crying. 'We have to leave. I'm scared I'm going to lose her. Or lose you. Or Arash.'

I pull out the plug. The crimson water gurgles as it swirls down the drain …

My breath is shallow and my chest feels like it is going to explode.

I need to talk to someone.

I need to let this out.

The meeting finally ends.

Back in our room, Maman rants about the baby and Abdul and how she can't believe this is happening all because he punched a stupid wall on Nauru.

I wait until she has her back to me, then slide my phone card out of my Science book into my hand.

I edge towards the door. 'Maman. I'll be right back, okay?'

She barely hears, but Arash looks at me with eager eyes. 'I want to come, Ana!'

'Not this time,' I say. 'Stay here. I won't be long.' I escape out the door before he can ask again.

KENNY

Jonathan is in the shower when I arrive home from work. I hear him chanting scraps of song, as spray thrums against flesh and floor. I walk towards my bedroom, then stop at a familiar sound.

Jonathan's ringtone: the chirp of R2D2.

I hesitate, then track the sound to his room. The phone is plugged into a charger by his desk. I pick it up and check the screen for a name. It reads: *No Caller ID*.

I make a split-second decision and answer it. 'Hello?'

There's a pause on the other end, then a female voice. 'Jono?'

'This is his dad. Who is this?' My mouth is dry.

'Anahita ... from school ... from Wickham Point ...'

JONO

I stop short as I see Dad standing in my room. He has my phone in his hand, pressed to his ear.

I panic. 'What the fuck?'

He doesn't even tell me off for my language, just holds the mobile out, looking stunned. I know it's probably Ana; she's the main person who calls me.

Adrenaline pumps through my veins, as I say, 'Hello?'

'Jono ... is it alright? Your dad answer the phone.'

I look up at Dad, but he doesn't move; he just stands there, glaring. I glare back and try to wave him away, which is awkward given the fact I'm still only wearing a towel.

'Sorry. I was in the shower,' I say.

'I ... my maman ... we had ... I want to tell you ...' She breaks off, her voice trembling with tears.

But Dad is scowling at me from the doorway, listening to every word.

'I'm so sorry, but is there any way I can call you back? Can I get your number?'

There's a long pause. 'I can't.' I feel terrible, as she hurries on, 'But I will see you at school.'

'Wait – Ana?' But she's already hung up.

I hurl the full force of my fury and guilt and disappointment at Dad. 'What the fuck are you doing in my room, answering my phone? Haven't you heard of fucking privacy?'

Dad is deadly calm, but there's a quiet menace to his voice. 'Why is she calling you?'

'Why do you think? She's a friend.'

'You said you told her to get lost.'

'That was ages ago.'

'So – what now? Is she your girlfriend?'

'That's none of your business!' I shake my head in disbelief. 'You can't just barge in here and hijack my phone then drill me with questions –'

'I told you to stay away from those people. She'll use you. She'll use me.'

He sounds so paranoid and ridiculous that I laugh. 'Oh ... oh, right. 'Cause we're so useful. Ha! So high up and connected.'

'You don't know what desperation is. She could be dangerous. Her family could be –'

'You sound crazy –'

'What do you really know about her?'

'What do *you*?'

We stand there, glaring at each other across the room.

Then I move forwards, herding him towards the door. 'Don't ever answer my phone again.'

I shut him out. I don't swear or slam the door. I just close it and brace myself, expecting him to start banging, demanding to come in.

But there is only silence. Then the sound of retreating footsteps outside.

ANA

I walk slowly back to my room, with a tight feeling in my chest. I'd wanted to pour my heart out, and Jono just cut me off. Was it something to do with his dad? Kenny sounded distant and strange, but he's always been friendly to me in person. Did he not like me calling Jono at home?

I reach the door, push it open and go in.

Maman is standing there, doubled over, as Arash watches wide-eyed from the mattress nearby.

I hurry to her side. 'Maman, are you alright?'

She's panting. 'Too hot, Ana. Too hot.' She stands upright, fanning her face with one hand, and I realise she's standing in front of the air-conditioning unit stuck high up on the wall. She props her other hand behind her in a triangle to support her lower back. Her belly bulges forwards, so round it could almost drop off her body like ripe fruit.

'Is it the baby?' I ask.

'Just get the temperature down!' It comes out as an angry bark.

'I'll ask the officer for the remote,' I say. I hurry out the door, to the officer's station, and am relieved to see it's Milly on duty. 'My maman … she is hot … can you make the air-condition colder?'

She hears the anxiety in my voice. 'Is she alright?'

'I don't know.'

Milly grabs the remote control for our room and quickly follows me back.

Maman is leaning over a chair now, moaning in pain.

Milly takes one look at her and says, 'She's in labour.'

'What?' I want to tell Milly that she can't be, the baby isn't due for weeks. But Milly's already on her radio. 'Code Blue. I need IHMS to room 17B in Surf. There's a pregnant woman in labour.'

Maman starts to wail in Farsi. 'No … I can't … I won't go … I need Abdul …'

I turn to Milly with pleading eyes. 'The baby's dad … Maman's boyfriend … is on Nauru. They said … we made application many times …'

'Sorry, but there's not much we can do now. This baby's on its way.'

Maman lets out a blood-curdling scream. 'No! I won't! I won't have the baby without him.'

Arash starts to whimper, terrified by Maman's desperate cries. I scoop him into my arms, as two nurses burst through the door.

They quickly check Maman over, then turn to Milly. 'Let's get her to the clinic. And call an ambulance now.'

I say, 'Wait ... let me come.'

Arash starts thrashing and screaming. 'Maman! Maman!' I struggle to hold him back.

Milly says, 'You can't bring him. Sorry, you'll have to stay here. It's really just supposed to be husbands anyway.'

Maman lets out another wail. 'Don't take me ... I want to wait for Abdul ...'

I watch helplessly, as they support her out the door.

JONO

I hide in my room, avoiding Dad. Anger is still coursing through my veins. I need to calm down, so I pull my pot stash from the shelf. I keep it in a carved wooden box Mum gave me when I was small, hidden under a pile of lucky Chinese New Year envelopes from Aunty Minh and relatives in Vietnam.

I roll myself a joint and light up. Feel my body start to relax, my heartbeat begin to slow. I blow the smoke out the louvred window into the yard, hoping Dad doesn't go outside and notice the waft of pot. When I've had enough I stub it out and hide the evidence back in the box, spraying Lynx deodorant around the room to disguise the smell.

Lara calls and, for once, I pick up.

'Dad reckons you have a girlfriend,' she teases.

'Dad's an arsehole.'

'Oh. Right. One of those days, is it?' She laughs, then cautiously adds, 'Mum's here, by the way ... if you want to say hello?'

'I don't.' Irritation floods back into my body, despite the fact I'm stoned.

'She's not that bad, you know. It's been good to be able to hang out. To ... reconnect. I wasn't sure about moving in here, but it's actually really nice living with her again.'

'Good for you,' I snap, and hang up.

Dad's car finally wheezes out the driveway. He's on night shift at the moment. All the easier to sneak out. I text Will, and we both skate to Ludmilla to meet up.

He can tell straight away that I'm on edge. 'Something happen?'

'Just Dad again. And Lara was crapping on about Mum.'

'Right.' He knows not to push.

'Where to?' I ask.

'I said we'd swing past Matty's house and drop off some stuff. He lives in Nightcliff. Is that okay?'

'I guess ...' I wish Ana would call me back, but I know she probably won't.

Will misinterprets my reluctance. 'You said you wanted to help – before you got all obsessed with your new girlfriend ...'

'I've told you: I'm not obsessed.'

'You can have the earnings, if you want.'

'Whatever. Let's just go.'

We skate up Dick Ward Drive, cut through Nightcliff, then cruise along the foreshore. It is busy with joggers and cyclists making the most of the cool of evening. Families dot the grass, eating takeaway meals from the food carts nearby. A group of long-grassers hollers at us in some language I don't understand. We ignore them and glide on.

Will turns off into a backstreet somewhere near the back of the Beachfront Hotel.

A tall skinny guy from the year above us appears on the steps of an apartment block, spots us and crosses the road. He scans the street, then buys a sandwich bag of pot from Will and tips us with a carton of iced coffee. 'Thanks, guys. Appreciate the delivery. Hey, what are you doing tonight? You should swing past the Ludshed. It's a new crash we found in Ludmilla. Awesome parties. There'd be heaps of customers too.'

'Yeah?' Will looks from Matty to me, but I shake my head. I can tell he's disappointed, but he waves goodbye, saying, 'Another night for sure.'

We skate back to the foreshore and smoke a doobie as we skull the iced coffee. Will chucks me the hundred dollars he got from Matty.

I throw it back at him. 'You don't have to do that. It's not like I did anything.'

'Thought it might cheer you up. We could go to Cas Mall. Buy you a phone from this century.'

'With a hundred bucks?' I manage a small smile.

'I'll put it on a card. You can pay me back later. Bet you could earn the rest with one trip to the Ludshed.' He pre-empts my objection. 'Not now. Another time. Let's swing past KFC. Hit Mel up for a free meal, then go and check out phones.'

I know Dad will ask questions if he sees me with a new phone. But right now I don't give a damn what he says or thinks or does.

I say, 'Fuck it. Why not?'

We scoff down greasy chicken, then stroll leisurely around the cool air-conditioned mall. It's strangely soothing; the shops are light and bright with the promise of shiny, new things. We pass a shoe store with the latest Nikes on display and stop to look.

Will nods down at my flapping Dunlops. 'Shoes would definitely be a good investment. Buy what you want – doesn't have to be a phone.'

I check the price tag and say, 'Let's keep walking.'

We pass a jewellery shop having a sale. A woman in a suit beckons us in, saying everything is thirty per cent off. Will tries on a chunky black sports watch that costs six hundred bucks, as I meander around. In a glass corner cabinet, something makes me stop. It is a woman's watch with a thin silver band, almost like a bracelet. The face is black, but instead of numbers there are stars. The sticker beside it says one hundred and eighty bucks.

Will appears behind me and nods at the watch. 'For your girlfriend?'

I shrug, making out as if I'm not sure even though I know it'd be the perfect gift.

He shakes his head. 'Man, you've got it bad. I mean, seriously, what's the point of buying her expensive stuff? It's not like you're going to get any while she's locked up in there.'

Will always talks about sex like that. Casual. Crude. He and Mel have done it; they've been together a year. Priya and I went out for six months, but didn't make it past third base.

'It's not about that,' I say.

But he just laughs. 'Your balls must be as blue as the fucking ocean.'

He's not completely wrong.

I think about it. Of course I do. I imagine how soft her skin would be under her uniform, on her stomach, her thighs, her breasts. And sometimes, lying in bed, I imagine Ana there, doing the things I used to do with Priya. The memory, the fantasy, is so rich and so real that every part of my body throbs.

But I'm not about to admit that to Will.

I borrow his credit card and buy the watch.

'You're crazy,' says Will. 'What about the shoes? And the phone?'

I imagine Ana's smile when I give her the watch. 'They can wait.'

ANA

The hands move slowly around the face of the clock above our door. Every minute is like an hour. The room feels sad and quiet. I lie beside Arash on my bed on the floor.

Maman's mattress is empty beside mine; there is a dip in the centre of it where she usually lies.

Arash's little body squirms against my belly.

I say, 'Arash. Try to relax.'

His voice is small in the dark. 'I want Maman.'

'I know. I do too.'

I rub gentle circles on his bony back, and his breathing gradually evens out, his body softening into sleep.

I loop my arms around him. Regret tugs at my heart. This is where I should be. Where I belong. With my family. Not rushing off to call a boy. A boy who must've heard the tears in my voice, but didn't wait to hear what I had to say.

I feel like an idiot. And I blame myself. If I'd stayed with Maman after the meeting, and tried to calm her down, would she have gone into labour at all?

'I'm sorry.' I whisper it aloud, into the gloom.

But there is nothing. No reply. Just the steady rhythm of Arash's breath; it smells doggy and sweet.

I say it again, louder this time. 'I'm sorry.'

A door bangs somewhere down the corridor.

For the first time since we were on the *Kingfisher*, I turn to a higher power.

'God ... are you there? Please let Maman and the baby be alright. If you do, I'll do anything ... anything you want.' I try to think of something to offer, and use the only bargaining chip I have. 'I won't spend time with Jono anymore. I'll focus on my family. I swear.' Tears stream down my face. 'God ... did you hear me? Please? Do we have a deal?'

For a moment there is nothing.

Then I hear footsteps in the walkway outside.

KENNY

I stop outside the door to room 17B. Milly waits beside me, as I check the list of boat numbers in the yellow fluorescent glow of the hallway light.

It is the girl's room. The girl and her mother and brother.

I don't want to see her. What if she smiles that too-familiar smile again? Or, worse, asks why I was awkward on the phone? Milly would want to know why she's calling me at home, and how that came about. And there's no way I want to explain.

I hand the skeleton key and torch to Milly. 'You do a few.'

'Sure.' She turns the key in the lock and pushes the door open. 'Head count.'

I hang back but, to my relief, the lights are already off and the room is dark. Milly shines her flashlight around and locates two body-shaped lumps on the mattresses on the floor. One medium, one small.

'Just two,' she says. 'The mum went into hospital today.'

Is that why the girl phoned Jonathan? I make a note of the mother's absence on the list.

Then, as Milly's closing the door, I can't help myself: I sneak a glance inside.

I could swear I see the gleam of black eyes, wide and scared like a possum's, staring at me from the dark.

JONO

We're late to school again, thanks to Will insisting on scoffing a second serve of eggs. The lady in the office doesn't even have to ask our names. She just sighs and hands us late slips and tells us to hurry to class.

I can feel the box containing the watch jiggling in my bag as we walk.

I can't wait to see Ana and give her the present and explain about last night, and find out what she wanted to tell me and why she sounded so upset.

I push open the classroom door, expectation swelling in my chest. But her seat is empty.

Turner gives us an irritated glance and waves us towards our desk at the back of the room.

As we slide in next to Mel, she says, 'Where's your girlfriend today?'

I shrug, uneasy. 'I don't know.'

ANA

Arash is strangely still. He doesn't run around the room in circles, or try to climb the frame of the bunk bed. He refuses to go to the Mess, doesn't even want to go outside.

I make two-minute noodles to eat in our room and read him stories to pass the time.

'Can't go over it ... can't go under it ...'

There's a knock at the door. I open it to Turban, the

Indian guard.

He's grinning so wide I can see he's missing a few teeth. 'Good news! Your mother had the baby this morning. It's a girl.'

I'm dizzy with joy and relief. 'So ... she's alright? Maman? And the baby?'

'Both fine.'

I could swear I hear angels singing. I squeeze Arash. 'A little sister!' I turn back to Turban. 'Can we see her? Can my brother come too?'

He nods. 'At two o'clock. Someone will come to take you to the hospital for an hour.'

'Thank you ... thank you very much.'

He gives me a wink. 'Thanks be to Allah, eh?'

My insides freeze at the mention of God.

I try to smile again, but my lips feel contorted and strange.

JONO

I peer nervously into the Intensive English Centre. I've never been up here before. It's not how I imagined. I thought all the students would look different, that I'd be able to tell they weren't from here. I thought the girls would all wear headscarves like Ana, but most of them don't.

An Asian woman in a business shirt looks up at me from a nearby desk. 'Are you okay?'

'I ... I'm looking for someone,' I say.

'Sure. Who's that?'

'Anahita. Shirdel.'

The woman nods and says, 'She's in my English class. But she's not here today.'

'What about Zahra? I don't know her last name, but they're friends.'

'Wait here a sec, okay?'

I hang in the doorway, feeling conspicuous. There's an article from the *NT News* stuck on the wall. I read it to look busy. It's about a student at our school: a girl from 'war-torn Africa' who wants to become a nurse.

Zahra appears in front of me. 'Yes?'

I waver under her intense gaze. 'Ana called me yesterday ... but I couldn't talk. She sounded upset ... and now she's not here.'

'Her mother have the baby.' Her voice is flat and matter of fact.

'What?' I'm stunned.

'You don't know? Her mother is pregnant. Anahita not tell you?'

'No.' I feel my face flush.

Dad's voice sounds in my head: *What do you really know about her anyway?*

'She doesn't like to talk about her past ... or life inside,' I say.

Zahra raises an eyebrow but doesn't comment.

My mind is reeling. 'How long will she be away?'

'I hope not too long,' says Zahra. '*Inshallah*.'

ANA

The hospital reeks of antiseptic and bleach. There are two officers sitting by the door of the maternity wing. The officer who brought us greets them, and they nod for Arash and me to pass. Inside Maman's room, the floor is scratched tan lino, and the walls a heavy dark blue. The whole space feels sad and worn. But there is light from windows on one side.

And there is Maman, on the bed. I hurry towards her.

She is resting, eyes closed.

Arash struggles out of my arms and hauls himself up beside her. Maman's eyes burst open and she yelps in pain.

He crawls closer anyway, until he is panting in her face, like a little puppy desperate for a pat.

'Careful!' Maman shoves him off the bed.

His face crumples. I quickly pick him up and stand by Maman's side. Her skin is pale and paper-thin.

Next to the bed is a see-through plastic capsule, with a tiny baby bundled up inside, only her face visible above the white latticed cotton wrap. I stare at her perfect little lips, nose, eyes. I melt. 'Oh, Maman. She's beautiful.'

A doctor bustles in, stethoscope draped around his neck. 'How are you feeling now, Mrs Shirdel? Have the painkillers kicked in?'

Maman doesn't respond.

The doctor tries again, slower and louder. 'Any pain? Sore?' He gestures to her abdomen, and Maman manages a small nod.

'Is she ... okay?' I ask. 'The birth is ... alright?'

'It was a pretty classic C-section.' I'm not sure what that means. The doctor peers into my face, searching for understanding. 'You know, a caesarean?' He mimes a straight slash across his belly and says, 'I reckon she could've had a natural birth, easy, but it was like she didn't even want to try.' He picks up the chart hanging on the end of Maman's bed. 'Have we got a name yet? For the baby?'

I put a gentle hand on Maman's arm. 'Maman, what is the baby's name?'

But she doesn't answer. Doesn't say anything at all.

Just stares out the window, into the light.

JONO

I send Ana a message, trying my best not to sound too awkward or surprised.

Zahra told me about your mum and the baby – congratulations!

She doesn't reply. And she's not at school the next day.

I send another message.

Ana, is everything okay? I'm sorry I couldn't talk – my dad was standing right there. Can you call again? Or give me your number?

Still nothing. Desperation seeps in. Despite my resolve to stay cool, I send another, then another.

Are you coming back to school?

Please just message me. Let me know you're alright.

Are you angry at me for some reason?

I understand if you can't call, but I'm worried about you …

Either she doesn't get them or she doesn't want to reply. I think about asking Zahra for an update, but it's humiliating to admit Ana hasn't been in touch. I wish I could ask Dad if he's seen her at work, but I know there's no way he'll tell me anything that helps.

I google: *visit Wickham Point*. It comes straight up. *Wickham Point Alternative Place of Detention. Contact details and visiting hours. Open seven days a week.*

I'm nervy as I call the number and wait for it to ring. A man with a sing-song Indian lilt answers and tells me that I need to fill out a visit-request form first. 'I can email it to you. You just need to provide your details, some ID and your friend's boat number.'

'Sorry ... what's a boat number?'

'Just ask your friend in here. They'll know.'

I give him my email address, thank him and hang up, then add another message to my growing, unanswered list: *What's your boat number?*

And then: *What is a boat number anyway?*

My questions glare at me from the screen.

KENNY

I take my time as I enter an incident report from this evening: two Rohingya guys climbed onto the roof of the Sand compound, demanding to see their case manager. The night manager, Scott, said to ignore them; they'd come down once it got dark. But it's night now, and they haven't budged.

I wonder what they feel up there, under the stars and the wide open sky.

I finish the report and am about to log off, when I see someone has lodged an incident report for KIN015. The girl's mother.

I click on the file. Fatemeh Shirdel's detainment history fills the screen.

The report says: *Attempt to abscond from Royal Darwin Hospital with baby. Escorted back to bed. Detainee did not resist.*

I scroll down. There are hundreds of requests to see her lawyer, her case manager, a doctor, a nurse. Requests to transfer her boyfriend from Nauru to Darwin for the birth. I don't have access to the boyfriend's file; the Nauruans have their own system. But I can see the files of the two children. I click on KIN016.

The girl's file appears, and I quickly scan down the notes.

There are no complaints about her behaviour. I almost wish there were. There is nothing about her life history or her claim for refugee status either; only the case managers have access to that.

I jump as the door squeals open, and Scott leans his head in. 'You done yet? I need you back out there on the floor.'

ANA

Another 2.00pm visit. This time Eliza is at the hospital when we arrive. She's chatting to the officers outside the maternity wing and looks up as we approach. Arash bounds into her arms. She carries him into the ward, along with a teddy bear she's brought for the baby with no name.

Maman doesn't take the bear, or acknowledge it, or even smile. Arash claims the teddy as his own. He makes it walk over peaks of white sterile sheet, as Eliza hovers nervously by Maman's side. She tries the usual string of compliments: *She's beautiful. So small. She looks like you.*

Maman is silent. Blank.

Eliza tries again, this time more direct. 'Fatemeh, I want you to know I'm sorry Abdul wasn't here. I haven't given up. I escalated the case to reunite you, but I haven't heard back.' When Maman doesn't reply, she says: 'At least they're letting you go home tomorrow. That's good news.'

Maman finally speaks; her voice is hard and grey. 'And then what? Where will they send us after that?'

I translate, and Eliza falters, 'Well, they can't legally send you back to Iran unless you agree. I'm sure your lawyer would've told you that –'

Maman cuts over her. 'What about Christmas Island? Or Nauru? They can send us back there, to hell on earth.'

Eliza doesn't need me to translate the Farsi this time; she understands Maman's bleak tone and the names of the detention centres. Her voice wavers with the threat of tears, as she replies, 'I have to be honest ... I don't know. But they don't generally send mothers anywhere until the babies are at least a few weeks old. And, in the meantime, I'll do everything I can.'

I translate for Maman, but from the look in her eyes I call tell she's starting to think that Eliza's 'everything' doesn't equate to much.

JONO

I hurry to catch Zahra as she climbs off the detention centre bus.

She fixes me with a no-nonsense gaze. 'Yes? What?'

I get straight to the point. 'I want to visit Anahita, but I haven't been able to contact her. Is she okay?'

'She is looking after her brother. Her mum is still in hospital.'

'Of course. I'm sure she's busy but ... Do you think she'd want a visitor?'

I'm about to ask about the boat number thing, but Zahra is already walking away. Brushing me off. She throws one last sentence over her shoulder as she goes.

'You want to visit – you ask her.'

I try to keep busy to stop myself dwelling on Ana's silence. Dad's on night shift again, so Will and I head out. We go to the shed in Ludmilla, the one Matty told us about. I haven't been there before, but Will's been once with Mac. They've been raving about it ever since. Will reckons it was the best party ever – plus he sold heaps of pot.

We skate up the main road, throw our boards over a low metal fence and climb over. Walk through bright green grass up to our knees. Nearby there's a smattering of rundown concrete houses, each painted in a different colour.

I recognise where we are: an Aboriginal community not far from our school. I've been past this place thousands of times, but never come in.

'Isn't this Bagot?' I ask.

'Kind of,' says Will. 'But we're not going there. We just stay in the Ludshed. No-one else uses it. No-one cares.'

We're close now. Music throbs through the metal door. Will pushes it, and then lifts to counteract a broken hinge.

Inside it's nothing special, just a dirty concrete floor and tin walls. It's big enough to have a bathroom area though, with two toilets sectioned off by a corrugated iron divider. Year 11s and 12s fill the empty shed, dancing and laughing and goofing around.

Matty appears from the crowd. 'You made it,' he says.

He does an elaborate handshake with Will that makes me wonder if Will's come more than once.

I look around again. 'Who owns this place anyway?'

'Dunno.' Matty turns to Will. 'D'ya bring more tonight? That last lot was the bomb.'

Will nods. 'Jono's gonna help with distribution.'

He gives me a wink. We start to sell and smoke and sell and smoke. Will jokes around, making small talk with the customers, as I take their cash.

He grins at the growing wad of plastic notes in my hand. 'What's next on your shopping list?'

'I've still got to pay you back for the last trip.' I think of Ana's absence and the watch lying in my drawer at home.

As if he's read my mind, Will asks, 'What's happening anyway? You going to visit her?'

'Yeah ... probably ... soon.'

'Have you even spoken to her?'

'It's hard – she won't give me her number 'cause

apparently it's tricky to get calls ... so I have to wait till she calls me and she hasn't done that since Dad answered and ... I don't know ... it probably put her off ...'

Will looks concerned. Protective, even. 'Jono, if she's messing you around ...'

'She's not.'

'I warned you, remember? I said be careful this time.'

'I know. But everything's alright. Her mum's just had a baby. I'm sure she'll get back in touch soon.'

'If you're sure.'

'I'm sure.' But we both know I'm not.

'Look, Jono, forget about the watch.' Will nods at the money in my hand. 'And you can keep that cash. Just promise me you'll buy something for *yourself* this time, okay?'

I know Will is worried; this is his way of trying to help. I hesitate, then fold the notes and shove them in my pocket.

'Thanks.'

ANA

I hold the tiny baby against my chest. She is as light as a carton of milk. We wait for the officer to unlock the Surf compound gate and let us in. Maman's eyes are blank. Her arms hang limply by her sides. She barely seems to notice Arash clinging to her skirt as if he's worried she might disappear again at any time.

The officer reaches out and checks the ID hanging around Maman's neck.

I hold out mine and Arash's, and one for the baby too. A new one made just this morning: KIN014.1

The officer's eyes flick over it. 'Baby got a name yet?'

'No.'

He peers at the tiny bundle of baby. 'Boy or girl?' I tell him, and he smiles. 'She's gotta have a name. What about … I don't know … Did you want something Australian? Tell you what's big at my kid's childcare centre at the moment. Emily. Or Molly. Or Mia. What about Mia?'

'Maybe.' I manage a polite smile.

He looks from me to Maman, who is staring at the red dirt under our feet.

'I think someone's gonna come with baby clothes and bottles and formula and all that. Did they give you that stuff already?'

Maman remains mute.

I say, 'No. Not yet.'

'They should be in soon then. I'll tell 'em you're back from the hospital.'

'Thanks.'

As we enter our small cube of a room, the baby starts to wail. Maman slowly lowers herself onto the mattress, grimacing in pain. I hold the baby out towards her. 'Maman, do you want to feed her?'

But she just rolls on to her side, facing away. Silent, like she was the whole drive here. Arash goes to lie beside her and presses himself against her back. I jiggle the crying baby, then start to sing.

You are the sky's great moon,
And I'll become a star and go around you.
If you become a star and go around me,
I'll become a cloud and cover your face ...

I see Maman's body tense, but she doesn't move or join in. It breaks my heart, as I remember ...

... Maman singing at a small private party in our apartment in Tehran. It is one of her favourite songs: 'Ghoghaye Setaregan' by Parvin. Her voice soars and dips, as my family swells around me. Aunties and uncles and grandparents and cousins, laughing and dancing and singing along.

Yasmin appears beside me, and puts a glass of orange juice in my hands. She whispers, 'It's got vodka in it.'

I stare at her, then start to laugh. Abdul got some alcohol on the black market for the party, but obviously it's not meant for us.

We take turns sipping it, as we laugh and dance. She throws her arms around me.

I wince as she touches my back. It's still painful and raw.

She says, 'Sorry ... sorry ... I'm just going to miss you so much.'

We're leaving tomorrow, and she's the only person I've been allowed to tell.

I hug her back, holding her tight, so tight ...

The baby lets out a bleating protest, then starts to calm. I keep singing.

If you become a cloud and cover my face,
I'll become the rain and will rain down ...

My cheeks are wet with tears, as my baby sister's tiny eyelids finally close.

KENNY

I hear them talking as I sign out. It's 5.45am, and the officers for the day shift are lined up on the other wall, waiting to go in. One of them catches my eye and gives a friendly nod. I should know his name, but I don't.

The man says, 'You were in Surf, right? Last night?' I nod, as he continues, 'Did you see that new mum? Just back from hospital yesterday. Won't even hold her baby.'

He seems to be waiting for a reaction, but I don't know what to say. An image flickers into my mind: Roxanne curled up in our bed at home, weeping, as baby Jonathan wailed from the bassinet.

The woman behind the desk says, 'It's just barbaric.

Who wouldn't want to hold their own baby? I tell you, these people.'

The man says, 'Apparently there's a big lot of 'em leaving soon – did you hear that? The ones who came here from Nauru to have babies are gonna be sent back.'

A droplet of guilt trickles down into my chest.

I tell myself I should be glad.

ANA

Zahra and her mother, Meena, come to see us early the next morning. I'm relieved that Maman at least sits up to receive her guests. Meena is all curves, from her hips and breasts up to her lips and eyes. She bustles around, restoring a motherly sense of order. She unpacks the baby supplies, which were delivered last night, and says, 'You girls take Arash to breakfast. We'll be okay here, won't we, Fatemeh?'

To my surprise, Maman nods. Meena's red lipstick curves up at the corners even more. She beams in my direction. 'Your mother tells me you're going to be a doctor. That you don't like to miss too much school. I'm happy to come and help her on weekdays. It would be my pleasure.' She picks up the baby and coos into her little face, before declaring, 'She looks hungry.'

Maman talks in low, pained mutters of Farsi, then lifts her top to reveal two swollen red breasts, so full and angry they seem to shine.

Zahra gives me a look. 'We'll go then?'

'Yes.'

I duck into the bathroom, and catch sight of my sunken eyes and scabby head. I quickly tie a headscarf on, remembering what it felt like ...

> ... walking off the plane in Malaysia, elation trilling in every step.
>
> Maman's face glows as she pulls her hijab from her head. Glossy brown hair spills out around her face.
>
> She grins at me. 'Take yours off, Anahita.'
>
> I do. It feels like I've removed a fiery iron band.
>
> It is almost like freedom ....

Zahra, Arash and I escape outside. The sky shines bright blue; it is close and clear from a recent downpour of rain. I feel like I can breathe again. Arash runs circles around us, as we walk slowly towards the Mess.

'So you'll come back to school tomorrow?' asks Zahra.

'I don't know.' I avoid her eyes; my steps leave wet thong shapes on the concrete path.

'Ponyboy's been asking about you.'

'Who?'

She nods towards Arash and gives me a pointed look. 'You know. Ponyboy.'

I catch on. 'Oh.'

'He said he's sent you a lot of messages.'

'I haven't had time to check.'

'He wants to visit you.'

'I hope you told him no.'

She shakes her head. 'You can tell him yourself when you return to school.'

'I'm not sure I'm going to. I just feel like I should focus on family. That's what matters the most. Not school ... or anything else ...'

We both know the *anything else* is Jono.

Zahra frowns her confusion. 'I don't understand.'

I tell her about feeling guilty for leaving Maman to call Jono, but she brushes my concern away. 'She was due to have the baby soon anyway. It's not your fault she went into labour that day.'

I tell her hesitantly, tentatively, warily about my bargain with God.

To my surprise, she just laughs. 'You don't think I haven't made about a million of those myself? It's not like you have to keep your end of the deal. God never does.'

'But Maman and the baby are well.'

She regards me sceptically. 'Does your Maman seem *well* to you?'

I can see her point, but I'm not sure I can renegotiate the terms of my bargain now.

She says, 'You know what God – and your family – would want? For you to stay at school and become a doctor or a scientist or an astronomer. Or an astronaut like Anousheh Ansari.'

I manage a smile.

She takes hold of my hand and swings it playfully as we walk. 'Come back to school, Anahita. And if you're still determined to keep your deal, then just don't sit with

Ponyboy anymore. You know we'd all love it if you sat upstairs at lunchtime again. Just, whatever you do, don't give up school. If you stay in here, you'll get depressed.'

I know she knows what she's talking about; her long sleeves brush up against my bare arm.

She pulls her ID card up over her head and holds it out towards me. 'Here. I've got computer time now. Go and check your messages, and I'll take Arash to the Mess.'

I hesitate, looking at her ID photo. 'What if they realise I'm not you?'

She scoffs. 'You really think the officers can tell two Iranian girls apart?'

She's right. I show Zahra's ID and walk straight in. When I log on to Facebook, a river of messages from Jono floods onto my page. The first lot are almost perfunctory. Congratulations and practical questions about how I am. But then worry seeps into his words. And then, the most recent ones aren't questions at all. I realise they are notes from our class. They've started the unit on the Big Bang. I read his carefully typed words:

The Big Bang according to Turner.
In the beginning there was nothing. The universe was just a small, hot mass. But then something happened. They don't know exactly what … (Or maybe I just tuned out during that bit) But maybe it was as small as two atoms connecting and bang! The mass expanded quickly … creating the stars and galaxies we see today … (Just like when I first saw you. Bang! ;-))

I feel my resolve to keep my promise to God slipping away.

JONO

I wait out the front of school, fiddling nervously with my phone. I'm determined to approach Zahra again, and find out Ana's boat number, even if it means begging. The detention centre bus turns into the school driveway. I pocket my phone and straighten my back. Peer into the windows, as the bus pulls up.

I spot Zahra … and Ana! My heart leaps.

I grin and wave at her through the glass, but she doesn't see. She files down the aisle of the bus behind Zahra, pausing to show the guard something as she gets off.

I take an eager step towards her. 'Ana – you're back!'

She looks up and sees me, but her smile, when it finally comes, is fragile and uneasy. Zahra quickens her pace and moves ahead. I hang by Ana's side, unsure what to say.

'How's your mum?'

'Good, thank you.'

'And the baby? Is it a boy or girl?'

'A sister.'

'What's her name?'

'We don't know. My mother is … she still decide.'

The chatter of students swells around us, as we enter the school. Talk about the weekend and parties and who kissed who and who went where. We reach the base of the stairs.

I try to sound confident as I say, 'See you at lunch then? Usual place?'

She takes so long to answer, that I am relieved when she finally says, 'Yes.'

Something has changed between us. Ana sits further away from me than usual, and barely talks as we eat our lunch.

I ask if she got all my messages, and she nods.

I force myself to ask, 'Then why didn't you reply?'

She shrugs, but I don't want to let it drop. I ask if she's angry at me for not being able to talk the night Dad answered my phone. I guess that she was calling to tell me about her mum having the baby. I say I wanted to talk to her – I wanted to talk to her so much – but Dad was hanging around, acting weird. I don't mention the fight that followed.

Ana shakes her head. 'No, not angry,' she says, and then nothing more.

I keep babbling to fill the silence. 'I got you a present actually ... I didn't bring it in to school today 'cause I didn't know you were coming back. Zahra said you might be gone a while, you know, because of the baby. But I can bring it in tomorrow. Will you be here every day now?'

'I think so,' she says. 'But I don't ... need any present.'

'I know.' I press my body back hard into the brick wall. 'I just saw it and thought of you, that's all.' Another awkward pause. 'I guess I could keep it for your birthday. When's your birthday?'

'April. The twelve.'

I try to sound cheery. 'Okay, well, that's pretty soon. I'll save it for then. If you're sure.'

I pull out my iPod and she tucks the earpiece into her ear. I play her the music I know she loves. The music she says is beautiful ugly. I want to ask again about her complete lack of contact, but I can sense tears around the edges of her, so I stay quiet.

As the school bell sounds for the end of lunch, the words well out of me. 'Ana, I can tell you're upset about something ... and you don't have to talk about it ... and this probably doesn't count for much but ... I really missed you ... and I'm happy you're back.'

She finally raises her eyes to meet mine and seems to see me for the first time.

Her voice wavers. 'It does count. Thank you.'

ANA

Eliza comes to fill in the paperwork for the baby's birth certificate.

It says: *Place of birth: Royal Darwin Hospital, Northern Territory*. The space for her name is still blank. Eliza taps her finger next to it. 'Have you had any thoughts? I mean, legally, you can take two months, but that seems like a long time to be calling her Baby.'

Arash rearranges himself on Eliza's lap, basking in her easy smiles.

Habibeh translates, then asks Maman in Farsi: 'Do you

want a name that's traditional or modern?'

Maman sits slumped in her chair, staring out the window, through the grid of wire.

'Anahita can choose.'

It breaks my heart. She's always been so proud of the names she chose for us. Anahita is the goddess of water, and Arash was Maman's favourite character from the *Shahnameh*, a national hero who saved Persia.

I say, 'What about Setareh?' It means star.

Maman's eyes flick towards me.

Eliza says, 'How do you spell that?' She writes it down on the form. 'Have you called Abdul yet? He must be thrilled.' Maman is silent, so Eliza looks to me. 'Anahita? Your dad?'

'He's not my dad.'

'Sorry. The dad of Setareh.'

'We have not called.'

Eliza's lip quivers with compassion. 'Well, you should do that. It would be good for your mum. For all of you.' She turns back to Maman. 'Are you eating? The officers said you've skipped a few meals.'

Maman practically spits her answer. There is venom in her voice. 'Eat? For what?'

KENNY

I see the young, blonde case manager, the one I saw before with the girl. She's pacing in the smokers' area. I hesitate, then approach. 'You got a spare?'

'Um. Yeah, okay. Sure.'

It's not until I get closer that I realise she's been crying.

She wipes her cheeks with the back of her hand, looking self-conscious. 'Sorry … it's just been one of those days …' She digs a cigarette from the packet in her pocket and holds it out towards me. Her hands are shaking. 'Do you ever get the feeling they hate you?' There's a laugh in her voice, but I can tell it's not a joke.

'Hate you? You mean them?' I gesture to the rows upon rows of rooms.

She nods. I take the cigarette and hold it awkwardly in my hand, wishing I'd thought of a different excuse to talk to her. It's been nearly twenty years since I last smoked; I gave up at the same time as Roxanne, when she was pregnant with Lara.

The woman forces a smile. 'I thought I could make a difference, you know? Working on the inside. You probably think that's pathetic.'

'No … no, not at all …'

There is something about her that reminds me of Jonathan. The way she doesn't seem to have a verbal filter or an emotional shell. I hate people crying. I never know what to do.

'Have you been working here long?' It's not like I really have to ask; if the tears weren't enough of a giveaway, her Department lanyard is still shiny and new. I've even overheard officers placing bets on which way she'll go. According to the old hands 'newbies' go one of two ways: they either harden or break. I wonder which way they bet on me.

'Just a few months. It's going really well, as you can see.'

She manages a sarcastic smile, but her eyes pool with sadness. 'How do you work in here every day?' She looks at me like she really wants to know.

I'm surprised to hear myself saying, 'I think about my son. I do it for him. So he never has to work somewhere like this.'

I realise I mean it.

She smiles again, and this time her smile is as warm as sunshine. She gestures to my still-unlit cigarette. 'You going to light that?'

I'm glad she can't see me blushing – there are some advantages to Asian skin. I look around and notice the safety lighter in a nearby post. I bend down to look at it, unsure how it works.

There's amusement in her voice, as she says, 'It's a bit like a car cigarette lighter. Just push the red button and stick the end in the hole beneath.'

I follow her instructions, grateful that she doesn't ask why I don't already know this. Smoke curls from the white tip of the yellow stick. I take a tentative drag. It's more bitter than I remember, but there's something familiar about it too. Comforting, even. I inhale again, this time deeper, trying not to cough. I'm sheepish, like a teenager trying smoking for the first time.

In between puffs, the woman says, 'I'm Eliza.'

'Kenny.' I try to sound offhand as I add, 'So, which families are you working with?'

'Which ones aren't I? The list feels this long!' She holds her hands a metre apart, her forced laugh betraying the fact she's overwhelmed.

'I think I've seen you with the Shirdels?'

She nods. 'That's who I just saw. Do you know them? I mean, I guess everyone knows everyone in here.'

'Not personally. But professionally, yes.'

She seems amused by my need to clarify. 'Of course.'

'What's their story? I mean, before they came to Australia?' I slide it into the conversation like it's a normal thing to ask.

But Eliza is suddenly wary. 'I, um, don't think I'm supposed to discuss their personal histories ... am I?'

I squirm. 'Well, us officers know a lot of it anyway ... but if you don't feel comfortable talking about it ...'

'They said it was confidential. In the training.'

'Of course. I was just curious. They seem so well-off – the way the mother holds herself, the makeup, the hair ... I didn't understand why someone like that would come here by boat.'

Eliza exhales her smoke away from me, towards the fence. 'Sorry, I can't say. Just got to be careful, you know? It's not like I can afford to get fired.'

I take another drag to hide my frustration. 'No worries. I understand.'

ANA

I settle Maman in the seat in front of the computer and open Skype. The camera is deactivated, as always, but the microphone works. Abdul answers the call straight away; I sent him a message to organise the time.

His voice is tinny through the speakers. 'Hello? Hello? Fatemeh? Arash? Anahita? Are you there?'

He sounds so far away. He *is* so far away.

Maman leans in towards the black monitor. 'I'm here, Abdul. We all are. We're here.'

Arash is by her side. He yells, as if trying to project his voice across the ocean to Nauru. 'I'm here too, Baba! I'm here too!'

We hear Abdul laugh and, encouraged, Arash yells again. 'I've got a little sister, Baba!'

There's a long gaping silence, then a ragged sob. 'A little girl. Praise, Allah. What's she called?'

'Setareh,' I say. 'Maman let me choose.'

Abdul says, 'Perfect. So I can see her every night.' There's another gasp, then: 'What does she look like? Our Setareh?'

I raise the sleeping baby up, then lower her again, remembering the camera doesn't work.

Maman is sobbing now, so hard she can't talk at all, can barely balance on her chair.

I gaze into Setareh's tiny, squished-up face. 'She's beautiful. Like Maman.'

Maman lets out a low, mournful moan.

JONO

I do everything I can to bring back the Ana from before, the one whose smile reached her eyes. I try to do more 'things that count'. I play new music, downloaded especially for her ears. I write out the lyrics to the Australian hip-hop songs she likes so she can understand all the words; I copy them down from my laptop screen in scrawling, looping pen until my hand aches like I've been in an exam.

I bring double-sized lunches to school to share, replacing my canteen-bought meat pies with Vietnamese food from home. Aunty Minh is ecstatic and starts bringing extra things over: sweet soups and sticky rice and spring rolls. She thinks I'm eating it all by myself, and cooks bigger quantities every time she's at our house for dinner. 'You eat good. Growth spurt. About time – too skinny.'

I just nod and smile and pack it away for tomorrow's lunch.

Dad has been brooding and distant since our fight. Apart from mealtimes, I avoid him and stay in my room, or go out to the shed to drum.

At first, it seems as if Ana barely tastes the food I bring. But as the weeks go by she starts to comment on things that are especially spicy, salty or sweet.

One day, I ask if there's any food she misses from home.

'My maman's curries.'

Her voice is filled with yearning.

ANA

I scoop the chicken and steamed vegetables into a napkin hidden on my lap, then twist the thin white tissue into a ball and tuck it into my sleeve. I want to sneak it back to our room for Maman, and mix it in with two-minute noodles so there's a chance she'll eat it. She hates the bland food in the Mess and, lately, refuses to come, saying it's too loud. She hears the scrape of plastic cutlery; the clang of metal from the serving area; even the chewing of food in mouths – she says it sounds like the saliva and gnashing teeth are right in her ear.

I look over at Arash, who is eating a plate of plain rice and sipping juice. I didn't have the energy to fight with him about eating a proper meal today.

Around us, rows of people sit eating and holding low, worried conversations. The mood is brittle, like something's about to snap. I tune in to the talk around me. There's been another attempted suicide, and more people have been moved in the middle of the night. Everyone's heard the heavy clomping of officers' boots, and the terrified screams as people are dragged out of their rooms and taken to the Sun compound. The rumours are that they're being sent to Nauru.

An older Iranian woman tuts. 'The poor babies, they're always sick on Nauru.'

Even the thought of Setareh on Nauru makes me want to scream.

Arash finishes his rice, and I stand. 'Let's go.'

'Ice-cream ... I want ice-cream,' he whines.

'No!' My voice is louder, angrier, harsher than I expect. He flinches, and I quickly try again. Softer this time. 'Arash, please, let's get back to Maman. She needs us. Come on.'

He reluctantly follows me towards the exit. I'm relieved to see that Kenny's stationed at the door, counting people in as others leave. I try to hurry past, angling my sleeveful of dinner behind my back.

Then I hear his voice. 'Wait. Stop.'

Arash disappears behind my skirt.

Kenny nods towards my sleeve. 'What's that?'

I look around. Blockhead is walking towards us from the bain-maries.

I whisper, quick and urgent: 'Kenny, please ... my maman won't eat ... she has baby ...'

'Take it out.' There is no trace of understanding or friendship in his voice.

Blockhead is by his side now. I inch the bundled napkin out of my sleeve and hold it out.

Kenny wrinkles his face in disgust. 'I don't want it. Put it in the bin.'

KENNY

I feel Rick nod his approval, as the girl throws the balled-up food into the bin by the door.

I hear myself saying, 'I don't know how you do things in your country, but here we have rules.' My voice doesn't sound like my own. It's a phrase I've heard Rick say, yet never thought I'd use myself.

But I don't want Rick asking me questions about the girl again, or accusing me of giving her special treatment, so I hold my ground.

The girl nods and apologises, even cowers slightly. And to my surprise it feels good. Good to be listened to. Good to have respect. The opposite of how Jonathan treats me at home.

She backs out the door and walks away. Her brother runs in front of her, then doubles back and tugs her hand. She shakes him off and keeps walking.

I feel a twinge of guilt.

Rick must see it in my face, because he says, 'Don't feel too bad, mate. Just a lover's tiff. She'll get over it.' There's laughter in his eyes, but his mouth doesn't smile.

I tell him to rack off.

JONO

In Science, we learn about galaxies and Edwin Hubble and radio telescopes and the expanding universe.

But despite Turner's encouraging smiles and prompts, Ana doesn't ask questions or even take notes. She just sits there, legs dangling, staring out the window.

I joke, 'Hey, you do a good impression of me.' But neither of us laugh.

I take notes on her behalf, hoping she'll read them at home. But I don't think she does.

I go to Cas Mall and buy her a packet of plastic glow-in-the-dark stars. The kind I had when I was little. The kind I got from Mum.

Will's given me his iPhone again, on permanent loan, so there's no need to save up for that. Still, remembering my promise to buy something for myself, I use the money from the Ludshed to buy myself the Nikes, then spend the leftover bucks on an external hard drive from JB Hi-Fi. It feels good to want things and just be able to walk in and buy them. Not have to wait or wish or plead with Dad.

I hand the stars to Ana at lunch, explaining that you can see them in the dark.

Her eyes light up. For the first time in weeks, she is luminous. Aglow.

ANA

I hover impatiently as Meena loads Setareh into the pram ready to take Maman to get her nightly sleeping tablets from the nurse. The bedroom door finally bangs shut behind them.

I crouch down beside Arash. 'You are not allowed to do this – understand?'

He nods solemnly, staring with big brown eyes.

I pull Jono's gift from my schoolbag, then climb up the metal frame so I'm the height of the top bunk. I hold on with one hand, reaching up with the other to stick the stars onto the ceiling, one by one. They are pale yellow, barely visible against the white concrete in the fluorescent light.

The thought crosses my mind that if an officer did come in now they might think I was trying to hang myself. Enough people have tried.

I look around, up high. How would you do it, anyway? There is nothing to attach to, nothing but the light fitting, and surely that wouldn't hold.

I climb down and tell Arash to close his eyes. He looks scared but shuts them anyway. I feel a pang of wonder-guilt; he trusts me so completely. I turn off the light. 'Now open them.'

I'm expecting a gasp of delight, but Arash sees the stars hovering in the dark and starts to whimper.

'No, Ana. No! I want to get off. Get off, Ana! Go home!' His little body is trembling with fear.

I quickly turn the light back on and wrap him in my arms. 'It's okay, Arash. I'm here. I'm here.'

I realise the last starry nights he saw were on the boat.

The ground seems to lurch beneath me ...

... as waves hurl me from side to side, crushing my body against Maman's. Abdul is beside her, vomiting over the side. I hold Arash tight, desperate to protect him as he sobs in my arms.

There are people everywhere around me, beside me, on top of me, hemming me in.

The stars above us are frozen and beautiful, but I am covered in sweat, and the air is full of the smell of sick and salt.

Daylight appears at the edges of our vision and slowly creeps in.

The stars fade into pale white-blue.

A man's voice yells out.

And suddenly everyone is calling, pointing up at the endless sky, crying and praising God.

Two white seabirds hover above us, floating on invisible currents of wind.

Maman has tears of joy in her eyes. 'Land must be close.'

I watch the birds as they dip to skim the water.

They are the most beautiful things I've ever seen.

I hug Arash to my chest and reassure him that we aren't on the boat, that we're never going to be on the boat again.

He gradually stops crying. I tell him I'll take the stars down, but he shakes his head and says to leave them up: 'For my sister, Setareh.'

That night, the pointy shapes glow down at us from above.

Maman's voice reaches out, soft and wary. 'Anahita, what is that? On the ceiling?'

'Stars, Maman,' I say. 'My teacher gave them out at school. We're studying the Big Bang. It was this huge explosion, how the universe began.'

For a long time, Maman is quiet. I hear Arash's breathing settle into the even rhythm of sleep.

Then Maman's voice searches me out again. 'I remember your father told me about this big explosion, before ... It is in the Qu'ran too. Heaven and earth were stitched together ... then they were torn apart ...'

She breaks off, and the room is silent again.

The stars fade into black.

I hear Maman sobbing softly in the dark.

In the morning, an officer appears at our door.

'KIN016? You have a birthday this month, right?'

I pause, confused, then nod; it must be the first day of April. The days and weeks have become a blur.

Arash jumps up and down; he's heard the word 'birthday' and knows what that means. 'Can I come? Can I come, Anahita?'

The officer smiles. 'Sorry. Just the birthday girl. What month's your birthday, little man?'

Arash doesn't understand, so I answer for him. 'October.'

Arash echoes, 'Tober.'

The officer lets out a long, low whistle and gives him a sympathetic look. 'That's a long time to wait.'

I say, 'I will stay here. I don't want cake.'

But he says, 'Come!' It sounds like an order.

I follow him to the common room, where a small group stands waiting with another officer. It's a random assortment of adults and teenagers and children from all the different nationalities: Iranians, Rohingyas, Hazaras, people from New Zealand and Vietnam. There is only one other woman I know: an Afghani Hazara woman called Maheen. She sometimes used to talk to Maman, back when Maman went to the Mess.

I move to Maheen's side, making polite conversation. 'What day is your birthday?'

'I don't know. I'm not even sure it's April. My passport was thrown overboard, and that's the month they gave me when I arrived. It doesn't matter anyway.'

We walk past the soccer fields to the Rec room and file in.

In the centre of the room there's a table topped with the biggest cake I've ever seen: an enormous white rectangle with green and yellow lettering proclaiming *Happy Birthday!*

The officer directs us to line up so we can have our photo taken, one by one, with the cake.

I whisper to Maheen. 'Do we get to keep the photo?'

'Of course not. They keep it in your file and give it to you if you get out.'

I hate that she says *if*, not *when*.

I'm at the front of the line now. I force a smile, and the flash explodes in my eyes.

The officer waves me on. 'In the other line now to wait for a piece of cake. We'll cut it up when everyone's had their photo.'

Ten minutes later I'm handed a piece of cake and instructed to eat it before I go back to my room.

I hope Jono will forget about my birthday, but of course he doesn't.

He says, 'We should do something to celebrate. I could bring in some cake. You said the twelfth, right? I think that's in the school holidays.'

He consults the calendar on the phone Will gave him. He's enamoured with it, finding any excuse to use it. He googles the bands we listen to, and shows me stuff on his Facebook and Instagram and Twitter. Sometimes we take turns playing games, seeing who can get the highest score.

He's transferred all his music onto it too. He gave me his iPod – to keep this time – but it's still in property as they check it all over again.

He finds the twelfth on his calendar. 'Yeah, it is. And it's on a Sunday anyway. Damn. I won't even see you ... unless you let me visit ...'

I avoid his eyes and don't reply.

He stares up the corridor, towards the window of blue sky at the end of the hall. 'Imagine if we could go somewhere ... out there. If we could have an ice-cream and go swimming at Nightcliff Pool. Or go shopping at Casuarina ... or to a party with dancing ... or to see some live music. How good would that be?'

I don't understand everything he says, but I recognise the verbs. They belong to another world. My former life in Iran.

Swimming. Shopping. Dancing.

Have. Go.

KENNY

I notice the shoes first. It's hard to miss them: they're blindingly white. I ask Jonathan where they're from.

He says, 'The op-shop in Millner. Lucky, huh? Can you believe it?'

I can't. Who has enough money to give brand-new shoes to an op-shop? I suppose it could be someone who works at Inpex – the mine – they're all loaded. But still ...

The next day I go into Jonathan's room to deposit a pile

of clean washing on the end of his bed and spot the external hard drive on his desk. I wonder if he'll try to tell me that came from the op-shop too.

I walk to the desk and flip his laptop lid open. It asks for a password. Damn.

I try some of the standard lazy-person's options like 1234 and 'password' and Jonathan's name and date of birth, but they don't work. I try band names from the posters on Jonathan's wall, but still no luck.

I close the lid and look around the room. Nothing else new or suspicious stands out.

I open Jono's bedside drawers, one by one. In the bottom drawer there's a small white box. Opening it carefully, I see a women's watch, delicate silver with a black face. I stare. Is this for the girl? I hope like hell it's not. But even if it is, where did he get the money from? Is he borrowing stuff from Will again? Or something else?

Is it possible that he took the job at KFC without me knowing? Surely not.

My mind charges through the options like an angry bull. Borrowing? Begging? Stealing? No. No way. Not my son.

I feel queasy, as I tuck the watch away, back in the drawer.

ANA

I watch Maman fade into herself as the days pass. She hardly eats, only forcing herself to swallow just enough that the officers don't put her on high watch. At night, she tosses and turns. I take her to the doctor, who prescribes Panadol but refuses to change her sleeping tablets to something stronger.

Meena finds her a bottle of them on the black market instead. The new ones knock her out. Part of me is jealous. I sleep fitfully, as dark images swamp my mind ...

... scar-covered arms ...

... blood-curdling screams in the night ...

... Maman clutching Arash, scared to put him down on the filthy ground ...

... handfuls of my hair coming away in my hands ...

I ask one of the medical staff if they can find a scarf to cover my head. They ask around the other Christmas Island detainees, and hand me one the next day. It is bright blue like the sky.

As I tie it on, my heart begins to weep ...

When I wake, Setareh is crying. Maman doesn't stir.

I change the baby's nappy and give her a bottle; the milk in Maman's sore, red breasts dried up weeks ago now.

She's stopped putting on makeup, and wakes with knots in the back of her hair. She doesn't bother brushing them out. She barely notices. Barely leaves the room.

She doesn't watch *The Voice* anymore either. The ABC News blares out at us from the TV every hour of every day. It is never good news. We learn that more families have been sent to Nauru, and there are more transfers to come.

Maman's convinced it will only be so long until it's us.

I remind her of Eliza's promise to do everything she can. But the weeks are disappearing so fast, and we both know that even firm ground can shift beneath our feet.

The school holidays inch closer. Jono refuses to let the birthday-outing idea drop.

'What about the excursions you said they go on? Couldn't I just come to one of those? I mean, if you're out somewhere and I happen to be there, who's going to care?'

I know I should say forget it, never, no way. But the idea is a pinprick of hope. A promise of escape.

Jono looks at me expectantly. 'So? Where do they take you?'

I'm forced to admit that I don't actually know. I haven't been on any excursions to Darwin. I've always been too busy with homework, or helping Maman, or looking after Arash, and now Setareh too.

But I remember Zahra telling me about the cinema in Palmerston.

Jono's eyes light up. 'Great. Can you find out what movie? And if it's on Sunday? And the time? I can get a bus in. Meet you there.'

I allow myself to imagine sitting next to him, in the glow of the big screen.

It seems so normal, so carefree, so fun, that I say, 'Yes.'

KENNY

I pace, as I wait for Jonathan to get home from school. I hope like hell there's a rational – legal – explanation for all the stuff. Or, if there's not, that he'll at least own up without me having to resort to empty threats. The last thing I want is another confrontation. I'm tired of Jonathan avoiding me. Freezing me out.

I hear the front door open then slam shut. There's a muffled thud: Jonathan tossing his schoolbag against the hallway wall. He enters the kitchen and nods hello.

I hang by the fridge, trying to act normal. Whatever normal is. I ask, 'How was school, mate?'

To my surprise, he smiles. 'You never say it right. It's not *met*, it's *mate*. Say it.'

I can't help but smile back. It's a game we've played since the kids were small: pronounce the word Aussie-style. 'Roof' is the hardest; I sound like a dog barking, no matter how hard I try. But I'm happy to play along. 'Mate.'

Jonathan says, 'Ay. Can you say *ay*?'

'Ay.'

'M-*ay*-te'

'Mate.'

He laughs and mimics me: '*Met.*'

I laugh too, on a high from the momentary reprieve from Jonathan's scowls and sulks and snipes. I can't bring myself to ruin the moment by asking about the hard drive or the watch.

I'm silently berating myself for my pathetic parenting, when he says, 'Hey, will you be at the markets on Sunday?'

'Of course. Who else is going to help Minh?'

'I'm thinking about riding over, like I used to do with Mum and Lara.'

I'm stunned. I tell myself I'll talk to him about the other stuff later. It can wait.

I beam at this new friendly version of my son. 'Your aunty would love that.'

ANA

Arash tells Zahra that I got to eat birthday cake, and he didn't get any and it's not fair.

She looks at me in surprise. 'It was your birthday?'

'Not yet. It was just that thing they do in the Rec room with the cake. My birthday's on Sunday.'

'You should've said. We should do something.'

I feel awkward, as I tell her I put my boat number down on the list for the excursion to the cinema in Palmerston.

She eyes me curiously. 'Really? I didn't think you went on excursions.'

'Well, Maman said I could and ... I haven't been ... and your mum said she'll help with Setareh ...'

Zahra puts a warm, reassuring hand on my arm. 'I think it's great you're going. I'll put myself down too.'

Arash starts jumping up and down. 'I want to come!'

Zahra says, 'Next time, okay? This movie's for big people.'

Guilt presses on my shoulders, pinning me down.

I speak in English so Arash can't understand. I tell Zahra

that Ponyboy is coming too, and spin a story about how I happened to mention it at school, and he invited himself along.

It sounds pathetic and made up. It *is* pathetic and made up.

I brace myself for a lecture, but Zahra just shrugs. 'If that's what you want to do.'

'You're not going to tell me off?'

'As long as *you* don't tell *me* off for this.' She slides an old mobile phone out of her pocket.

I stare. 'Where did you get that?'

She avoids answering and says, 'I'm taking photos of all the babies. I want the media to know they're in here. Can I take one of Setareh?'

I nod, too stunned to question her or object.

She takes the photo and gives Arash a special wink. 'This is a secret, okay? Don't tell your mum.'

Arash nods. 'Oh yes. I know secrets.'

Zahra and I laugh. But I feel uneasy, as she hides the phone back in her pocket.

'Are you sure about this?' I ask.

She meets my gaze. 'You cope in your way, I cope in mine. Are you sure about the movies?'

'Yes,' I say. 'I need this.'

She nods. 'Then fine.'

JONO

I make my way through the bustle of bodies. Rapid Creek Markets is in full swing.

Dad spots me in the crowd, and his face lights up. He says, 'Where's your bike?'

'Locked it in the car park.'

He nods his approval; he's always paranoid about things getting stolen, probably 'cause we can never afford to replace them.

'I thought it might be too small for you,' he says.

I shrug. 'Small's okay – better for doing jumps.'

Aunty Minh grins at me from behind her table of newly plastic-bagged vegetables from our garden. 'Jonathan. You come. Good. Good.' She calls to a woman at a neighbouring stall in Vietnamese.

The woman smiles and says something back. Then, seeing my blank look, she teases: 'You no speak Vietnamese?' She says something to Dad in a playful, chiding tone. It seems almost as if she's flirting. I try to see Dad with new eyes. He's in his element here today; laughing and joking in Vietnamese. He reaches a hand up and rests it on my back, near the nape of my neck. He's short compared to me, but I guess by Vietnamese standards he's average. His face is handsome and smooth, his hair shiny, black and thick; a lot of other dads I know – like Will's and Mel's – are already balding.

He beams at the woman, switching to English: 'Jonathan's very smart. I always tell him – he can do anything he likes – as long as he studies and stays away from trouble.' He gives me a significant look.

The woman smiles. 'Maybe doctor.'

To my surprise, Dad shakes his head. 'No need to be a doctor. We already have one. Remember I told you? His big sister is studying Medicine this year. And Jonathan – he likes music and words. He's very talented that way.'

I'm stunned. I've never heard him say anything like that before. I feel a strange burst of pride.

Dad hands Aunty Minh his bumbag containing change for the stall, and turns back to me. 'Let's go for a walk. I'll buy you breakfast. Whatever you want. What do you like? You still like sticky rice? Something sweet?'

He guides me down the crowded walkway, his hand still on my back, like he wants to show me off.

He says, 'You know, if you need money, you can always ask me, right? You might not be able to buy everything you want, and I might not have the money straight away, but if it's important I'll find it for you, okay? There's no need to ... you know ... do anything crazy ...'

I have no idea what he's talking about. 'Sure.'

I could swear I smell cigarette smoke on his breath and his clothes, but that's impossible; as far as I know, Dad's never smoked in his life. I steal a glance back at the woman with the teasing eyes. 'Who was that?'

'Phoung. You know, your aunty's friend.'

'I think she likes you,' I say.

Dad laughs, but seems quietly pleased. 'No, no, no ... just friends.'

ANA

Jono is standing in the foyer of the cinema holding a bucket of popcorn in one hand, and a heavy-looking plastic bag over his other arm. He is wearing a faded black T-shirt with white writing scribbled on it that says *Nirvana*, and ripped black shorts, with a belt for once. It is the first time I've seen him out of school uniform, apart from in photos on Facebook. His clothes are shabby. Doesn't he have any pride?

But the thought exits my mind as he looks up and our eyes meet.

His gaze is hopeful and ridiculously sweet.

I smooth down my clothes, wishing they were more *me*, or at least the right size. I've put in a request with the guards for some bigger clothes, but they haven't arrived. My yellow T-shirt is so tight it shows the outline of my fraying bra and the hint of scars on my welt-covered back. Luckily, Jono doesn't seem to notice. He grins at me from across the room.

I give him a self-conscious smile as I follow the officers in. They walk straight past Jono. To them, he is just another movie-goer. He shuffles in behind us, showing his ticket to the usher. I sneak a glance back, and he nods towards the officers, widening his eyes, as if to ask: *what now?*

I don't know what to tell him. I imagined the officers sitting up the back, letting us watch in peace. But they stay right beside us, flanking us in.

I try to hang back, but Milly directs Zahra and me into the row of seats with the others, then sits down beside me.

My heart is thumping so loudly the whole cinema must be able to hear.

From the corner of my eye, I see him hesitantly slide into a seat two rows behind.

I could swear I can hear the crunch of his popcorn in my ears.

JONO

She looks really hot. She's wearing a tight yellow T-shirt that shows off all her curves. It is agony. If I climbed over two rows of seats I'd be right beside her. And in a security guard's lap.

I don't want to get her into any kind of trouble, so I hang back. I'm too distracted to watch the trailers. We swap smiles and glances across the space between us. Is this what the whole date is going to be like? I'd imagined us kissing in the dark. Hands wandering. Fumbling. Or, at the bare minimum, I thought we'd be sitting together. I've brought a whole bagful of market food, and a seriously overpriced bucket of popcorn from the candy bar out the front. Is she even going to be able to eat it?

I shoot her another look. *What's going on?*

She shrugs, apologetic, but doesn't move.

I chuck another piece of popcorn in my mouth and wait. And wait. And hope.

ANA

I glance back at Jono for what seems like the hundredth time, but is probably only the fifth.

Milly catches me looking, and asks, 'You know him?'

Zahra jumps in to help. 'He is at our school.'

'Friend of yours?'

My heart leaps into my mouth. But I don't want Zahra to be told off, so I say, 'He is *my* friend.' Milly raises an eyebrow, as I hurry on: 'We're in Science together at school.' I try to calm my nerves. Milly has no way of knowing that this was planned. And as long as she thinks Jono just happens to be here, we can't get in trouble ... right?

Milly asks, 'Does he want to sit closer?'

I stare, as she moves one seat over and waves Jono forwards.

He looks behind him, checking she isn't waving to someone else. There is no-one else. The cinema is practically empty.

My nerves are on fire, as he walks gingerly around the end of the row and down the aisle.

And then he's next to me, offering his popcorn to Milly with a sheepish smile, then passing it along to me and Zahra and the other detainees. My stomach flip-flops, like the popcorn is bursting inside my belly.

Zahra leans forwards. 'What's in that bag?'

Jono grins. 'A three-course meal. Popcorn is the starter. For mains there's roti and curry from the markets. My aunty has a stall there, remember?'

I nod. 'She sells vegetables.'

'Yeah. I stopped there this morning and got this. It's probably not as good as your mum's cooking, but it should taste alright.'

I can feel Zahra staring at the familiarity of our exchange, the way words flow between us like water.

Jono carefully extracts a tall stripy cardboard cup with a plastic lid from the bag. 'And this is dessert. Mango and lime. I didn't know which juice to get. There's so many options. I'll take you there one day so you can choose for yourself.'

My breath catches in my throat. *One day ... please let there be a 'one day', God ... please.* But I know God is unlikely to make any more deals with me. And there's a good chance the only *one day* I'll get is here and now.

I try to soak it all in. The silky blackness of the enormous screen. The velvet armchairs beneath my thighs. The smell of curry wafting in the air.

I can almost make-believe I'm at the cinema in Iran.

I can almost make-believe I'm free.

Jono thrusts the cup into my hands.

Beside me, Milly shakes her head, but doesn't intervene.

I take a sip of juice. A cold, sugary tang runs down my throat, through my chest, into my belly.

An icy sweetness.

JONO

The trailers finally end, and the cinema darkens as the movie starts. I quickly pack the food away for later. The plastic bag rustles loudly, and the guard shoots me a warning look.

I sit back in my seat, and turn my attention to the screen. I can feel the warmth of Ana's presence radiating from beside me in the semi-dark. I wonder if it might be okay, if she would mind, if anyone else would see, if I reached out and held her hand.

The thought strikes me as kind of ridiculous; I've done so much more with other girls.

But Ana isn't other girls. With her, even the small things feel huge.

I inch my hand towards the armrest.

ANA

His curled fist is resting on the cushioned arm between us, like a cautious brown mouse. Then it suddenly drops onto my knee. I startle but quickly try to regain my composure, checking that Milly and Zahra haven't seen. But we're well into the movie now, and everyone's gaze is glued to the screen.

I feel Jono nudge my arm, his brown puppy-dog eyes seeking out mine in the gloom: *Okay?*

I nod. *Okay.*

I feel his fingers weave into mine and forget everything else other than that his hand is warm, so warm.

I can feel his heartbeat in my palm.

JONO

She doesn't let go until the credits are rolling. She has been holding my hand so tight that when she finally eases away I can still feel the imprint of her grip on my fingers.

Our eyes meet in the flickering light.

I wonder what would happen if I leant forwards and kissed her. I ache for it. Well, that and more.

I inch forwards in my seat ... and feel her warm breath on my cheeks, my lips ...

Zahra's face appears from behind Ana's back.

I quickly sit back in my chair, glad she can't see me blushing in the gloom.

Zahra nods towards the plastic bag of food on the ground. She puts one finger to her lips and motions for me to slide it towards her. I nudge it over with one foot and watch, bemused, as she stealthily plucks a few things out and shoves them into her bag. Ana looks as though she's cringing, and for a moment I wonder if she knows I wanted to kiss her and is repulsed by that thought.

But then she snaps at Zahra in Farsi, and I realise she's embarrassed about the food. I feel stupidly relieved. I want to tell her it's okay, people take food all the time; my grandmother, Mum's mum, stuffs food in her handbag every time she's at a buffet. But before I can say anything, the female security guard stands up. 'Alright, folks, show's over. Let's go.'

I had forgotten she was there.

As we file out of the cinema, I remember the watch.

I dig the small, white jewellery box out of my bag and

press it into Ana's hand. 'I almost forgot. Your present. The one I bought ages ago.'

Panic enters her eyes; she stands there holding it like it's a bomb.

Zahra sees and snatches it off her, shoving it into her bag the same way she did with the food.

'We are not allowed.' Ana nods towards the guard.

I understand and don't, at the same time.

In the foyer, I say, 'Hey, we should get a selfie. To remember today.' I move in close next to Ana, waving for Zahra to get in too. I pull out my new phone, the one I got from Will, and hold it up. The screen is huge, compared to my old phone, and so clear. I flip the camera to face us, but Ana isn't smiling. In fact, she looks terrified.

'No photos allowed.' The guard's voice is right beside me. I startle in fright, dropping the phone.

I hold my hands up, as if surrendering. 'Sorry. I didn't know ...' I indicate the phone. 'Can I pick it up?'

The guard nods. 'But no photos, okay?'

'Okay. Sorry. I just thought ... to remember Ana's birthday ... it might be nice.'

The guard's eyes seem to harden as we say goodbye.

ANA

Milly waits until we're loaded back onto the bus before coming to talk to me and Zahra. She rests one knee on the seat in front of us, and fixes me with an accusing gaze. 'You made me think it was a coincidence that boy was there.'

'It was,' I say.

She shakes her head in disappointment. 'He said it was an outing for your birthday.'

'I only tell him now. Today. I tell him today it is my birthday.'

But she clearly doesn't believe me. 'I'm going to have to write an incident report about this.'

I feel like I'm about to vomit but force myself to say, 'Please. Only for me. He is *my* friend, not the friend of Zahra.'

Milly's voice is quiet and resigned. 'Okay.' She moves back up the front of the bus and takes a seat.

The other detainees are watching us, wondering what the hell is going on. I smear my tears away with blurry fingers, trembling as I remember ...

... the Nauruan immigration officials asking us question after question.

It goes for hours, until we're so tired that we can barely see.

Maman tells them we've already been through this twice on Christmas Island, but they insist on hearing everything again. She tells them about the whipping, and they request to see my back. I lift my T-shirt to show them the scars.

The Farsi interpreter seems to struggle to translate, as Maman explains about the morality police and the government and our constant fear ever since Baba

was killed and left by the side of the road.

They ask how long Maman has been with Abdul.

Abdul says, 'Many years. Our son is already three.'

But the officials aren't convinced. Maman and Abdul aren't married, and Arash's birth certificate was thrown overboard on the way here. They tell us 'some people' pretend to be together because they think it will help them get a visa.

Abdul argues and justifies and rants, until he loses his temper and slams his fist into the wall. The impact of it is so strong that it leaves a hole in the plaster. Abdul backs away, saying, 'Sorry … sorry …' But it's as if no-one hears.

Security rushes to restrain him, as Maman screams in protest …

In the bus Zahra puts an arm around my shoulder, but there's nothing she can say. We both know the terrible repercussions a record of bad behaviour on your file can have.

As we get closer to Wickham Point, she remembers the gift from Jono in her bag. She pulls out the little white box and flips open the lid. Despite the thrumming in my temples, I catch my breath. It's a beautiful silver watch with tiny diamond stars marking the spots where the hours would be. But I can't take it now. 'Throw it out the window.'

'Don't be stupid. Just put it on.'

'I can't. The metal detectors.'

'So what? I wear a watch. They'll never know you normally don't.'

My heart drums out a warning, but I let her strap it to my wrist. It feels like it's burning into my skin.

As the bus turns into the detention centre driveway, I wonder why I'm doing this, taking another stupid risk.

But I'm too numb to fight it now and, anyway, it's too late. We show our IDs as we file off the bus. And, to my searing relief, Zahra's right: the metal detector doesn't sound and no-one notices the watch is new.

Back in Surf compound, Zahra leads me to her room and tells me to wash my face before going back to mine. I follow her instructions as she says, 'Don't tell your mum about this, okay? She'll only worry and, you never know, Milly might not even record it. She's always been one of the nice ones.'

I nod, but we both know that even the nice ones have to follow procedure.

My mind frets. 'What if Maman finds out from someone else? Eliza? Or someone who was on the bus?'

'I suppose your case manager's a risk. But apart from her, your mum barely talks to anyone else except my mum.'

She pulls the plastic bag of food from her bag. I stare as the remnants of our feast reappear: two low plastic containers quarter-filled with curry and a paper bag containing the torn remains of flat bread.

'Here,' she says. 'Take it for your mum. But wait till my mum goes.'

I want to take it, but I'm worried. 'Maman will want to know where the food is from. And what if she notices the watch?'

As usual, Zahra is one step ahead. Her eyes flare with calm defiance. 'Blame me if you want. Tell her I got it all for you on the black market for your birthday.'

KENNY

I have a quick smoke in the staff car park before my shift. I buy my own cigarettes now. They're expensive, but I don't want to become known as a 'seagull' – someone who's always taking handouts.

I file into work and sign on with a sigh. Get my things: keys, ID, radio phone.

I fidget through the team meeting, then enter Surf just as the sun is starting to go down. I stop in at the staff computer room, and have a quick look at the girl and her mother's files. It's become almost a compulsion. I check at the beginning and end of every shift, hoping that one day I'll see a note. Something that says they're being moved away from Wickham Point. Away from my son.

I look up KIN014 first. There's nothing new. So I check KIN016. There's an incident report logged by Milly, which is strange. Someone like Rick submits reports complaining about detainee behaviour every other day, but Milly hardly ever does. I click to open it up, then read.

My breath quickens.

It's a report about an arranged meeting during the cinema excursion with a non-detainee boy.

I don't need to ask who that is.

ANA

I take the flat bread out of the white, greasy bag and hold it out towards Maman. 'Please eat. It's like naan, like we used to get at home.'

A glimmer of recognition flickers across Maman's face.

I put a piece of bread in her hand and say, 'There's curry too.' I spread the meal out before her. She stares at it like it's something from another world, then slowly raises the piece of bread to her lips and takes a bite. Her eyes fill with tears as she chews. She scoops some curry onto the bread, then takes a second bite, and a third.

Arash jumps impatiently up and down on the mattress beside us. 'I want some! I want some!'

I wrestle him into a hug. 'Arash, just wait. It's important that Maman eats.'

Maman divides the remaining piece of bread in two, and hands the bigger piece to Arash.

I tug it gently out of his grasp. 'Arash, give that back to Maman. Please. I'll take you to the Mess. You can have ice-cream.'

'Yes! Ice-cream!' Arash scrambles up. I hurry to follow.

As we reach the door, I hear Maman's voice. 'Anahita ...' I turn, on edge, ready to be interrogated about where the food came from, or how I have a new watch. But instead she just nods. 'Thank you, *azizam*.'

She just takes another bite and chews slowly, closing her eyes.

My heart sings. 'Keep eating, Maman. We'll be back soon.'

KENNY

I see her outside the Mess with her little brother, trying to stop him running up and down the line.

She calls, 'Arash! Officer! Officer!' He sprints to her side and peers anxiously around.

I try to reassure myself: no-one knows that the boy who met her at the cinema was your son. It's nothing to do with you. Just act normal. Breathe.

The girl slings a protective arm diagonally across her brother's thin chest.

I stop dead. There's something on her wrist. The watch I saw in Jonathan's drawer. The watch he probably stole. Did she ask him for it? Or bribe him? Or tell him to steal it?

I should've asked him about it straight away, as soon as I found it. I shouldn't have let it slip, won over by his rare friendly smiles. But it's too late now. He got the watch from God knows where, and now he's given it to this girl.

They'll manipulate you ... manipulate him ...

A protective fire ignites in my belly as I imagine her using his weakness for her gain.

The dragon rears up.

I take a step, then startle as Scott's voice rings out behind me. 'Kenny, I thought I asked you to do the room checks with Rick.'

My exhalation is hot and ragged. 'Just heading there now.'

I force myself to walk away.

Rick is waiting just outside the first room on today's list. He insists on doing the video recording; I'm lumped with the search yet again. I'm usually meticulous, but today I just do a general sweep. The room is all clear, but as we're leaving Rick points to a twenty-cent piece on the floor by the bed.

I pick it up and glare at him. 'Thanks, Rick.'

We complete the rest of the room searches, then I spend half an hour typing up a report for the twenty-cent piece.

I don't see the girl again.

As I sit, killing time on the computers at work that night, I feel wired and wild and wide-eyed.

JONO

My eyes snap open. Dad's face is right above mine. His hand is shaking my shoulder, and there's a barrage of words in my ear. I shrink back into the bed. 'Dad. Stop yelling.'

'Get up!' He moves a few inches back.

'What time is it?' I scramble to sit up.

He ignores my question, eyes blazing. 'You went to the movies with that girl. And you gave her a watch. I told you to stay away from her.'

I start to shake my head, but anger spews out of him like fire.

'Don't lie to me, Jonathan. I know you did it. Was it her idea for you to go to the movies?'

'What? Have you been spying on me?'

'Where did you get the money?'

My mind struggles to keep up with the barrage of questions.

'Did you steal it?' he asks.

'No.'

'Did she ask you for the watch?'

'No, I –'

'Or other expensive gifts? They sell them on the black market, you know. They're not sentimental about stuff like that. Personal belongings get traded all the time.'

I can't help myself. I say, 'She wouldn't do that. It was a present for her birthday.'

'Ha! I bet she made you think she actually cared. That's how these people operate. She'll use you and throw you away.'

I feel a lurch of doubt, then tell myself that Dad is crazy and none of this is true.

He continues. 'And you'll be left and ... you'll feel ...'

'What? Pathetic? Weak?'

I see a flash of guilt, then he turns and looks around my room. 'What else are you hiding? What else have you stolen? I saw the hard drive –'

'I saved up.'

But he doesn't even hear my lie. He's opened the cupboard and is pulling out my clothes, throwing them on the floor.

I beg him to stop. 'Dad, please. What are you doing? There's nothing here.'

'Where did you really get those shoes from?'

'I told you – the op-shop.'

He pulls the drawers out of my desk, and empties them, one by one, onto me, onto my bed, onto the floor. My stuff is everywhere.

'Dad! Stop! I haven't stolen anything!'

But there's a look of vindication in his eyes. I realise he's seen the smartphone charging on the floor. He picks it up and shakes it angrily in the air. 'Where did this come from then? Huh? Huh?'

'It's from Will, remember? He loaned it to me before –'

He lets out an angry primal kind of roar. His free hand swipes at the shelf above my desk. My row of dusty soccer trophies flies into the air, along with the carved wooden box from Mum.

I hold my breath, as the trophies clatter onto the floor.

The lid of the box snaps open as it lands. Its contents scatter across the light grey tiles: faded red Chinese New Year envelopes, cigarette papers, a lighter, a half-smoked joint and fat heads of pot.

I'm screwed.

KENNY

I pick up the marijuana and various bits and pieces, and put it all into a green plastic Woolworths bag.

This is even worse than I thought. He's out of control. I have completely lost control.

'You said you wouldn't smoke anymore.' It sounds lame, even to me.

'I don't. Much. I'm ... minding it for a friend.'

Of course, I know he's lying. I confiscate the shoes and the hard drive and the phone. My mind races: is this how he got the money?

'Have you been selling this marijuana?'

'No ... Dad, no ... 'course not.'

But his expression is as guilty as hell.

I want to shake some sense into him. Or beat him with a chopstick until he understands how serious this is; how it could destroy his future. I'm sure Will is involved, but there's no point talking to his mum. I think about calling Roxanne, then imagine her patronising tone as she explains what to do next.

I decide to call Minh, and ask her to come and stay with Jonathan tonight, while I'm at work. 'Can you come over by five? That's when I have to leave.'

She starts asking questions, of course. 'What has Jonathan done now? Is he crying again? Girlfriend break up with him?'

'No.' I try to keep the snap out of my voice; there's no-one else I can ask to help. I used to feel like I had friends here, but they've gradually faded away since Roxanne left. I guess they were her friends, really, not mine.

'I'll explain later, okay? Just come here at five, and make sure he doesn't go anywhere. You can sleep in Lara's old room. Can you do that?'

Minh agrees, and I hang up. I can sense Jonathan's

presence, as he listens sullenly from his room.

I yell down the hallway. 'Did you hear that? From now on, no going out. If it's a school day, I'll drop you there and pick you up. And if I can't be here I'll ask Minh to babysit.'

'I'm not a baby.' His voice is small.

I holler back at him, fury infusing my words: 'You act like a baby, you get treated like one.'

ANA

Maman sits in the shade of the walkway, cradling Setareh in her arms. It is the first time I've seen her hold her in weeks. Meena's sick today, so I stayed home from school to help. As much as I wanted to see Jono, it's almost a relief. My whole body tenses every time I think of the black mark on my file.

Through the fence in front of us, we can see a group of men playing soccer on the sports field. Arash has his own ball and kicks it against the fence, imitating the main game and whooping gleefully whenever he scores a pretend goal.

I sit next to Maman, taking it all in. The bright clear sky. The wet green grass. Dragonflies hovering everywhere I look. The air is less sticky today, and I wonder if the cool change Jono keeps promising is finally on its way.

For a long time, we sit in silence.

Then, to my surprise, Maman speaks. 'Your dad was a good soccer player. Do you remember? I used to take you down to watch.' Her voice is dry and scratchy from lack of use. 'I still think about him every day, you know.'

'I do too.'

'Sometimes you seem angry, like you think I met Abdul and erased your dad from my heart.'

'I don't think that,' I say.

But she doesn't seem to hear me. 'Maybe you'll understand when you're older. Maybe you won't. Love can arrive unexpectedly. You don't get a say in when or what or who. All you can do is grab it when it appears. And you do have to grab it. There's so much darkness in the world ...' Her voice trembles, and she breaks off.

I think about telling her about Jono and listening to music and going to the movies and holding hands.

But the news of the incident report would crush any shred of hope she might still have.

So I just sit beside her, watching Arash kick his ball against the fence.

A dragonfly settles on my arm.

KENNY

I drive to work with my shoulders as tense as steel. I break my own rule and light a cigarette in the car, inhaling angrily before hurling the smouldering butt out of the window, onto the gravel on the side of the road.

I blame the girl, of course. I blame her for all of it: Jonathan lying, sneaking around, selling marijuana, buying her gifts.

And beneath that, I blame myself. Why did I ever tell her

his name? Why was I so stupid as to get Jonathan involved in a mess like this? Particularly after last year – when he was so vulnerable. Weak. I know he hated me saying that, but it's true: when I hurt I harden, but he collapses into mush. The girl must've taken advantage of that. My son, the easy target.

In the team meeting, I barely hear the briefing, only tuning in at the word 'Iranian'.

Three families need to be moved from Surf to Sun compound in preparation for being transferred out early tomorrow morning.

Hope surges in my chest. But when the boat numbers are read out there are none that I recognise, and when I stop by the computer room to do my regular check there's nothing new on the girl and her mother's file. Damn.

I step out into the compound, feeling as though I'm moving in fast-motion, or have downed too many Vietnamese coffees. I scan the area, feeling paranoid, as I walk.

The atmosphere seems fraught, electric, on edge. But maybe that's just me.

And yet ... I could swear people are whispering.

Conspiring.

I see Milly escorting two women and a baby down the walkway.

The air rumbles with discontent.

ANA

As we walk back to the rooms, I hear a shout, then a panicked cry. I can't make out the words.

Some men I saw on the soccer field sprint towards the compound gate, where people are gathering. There are two women in the centre of it. Jamileh and Shadi, who is holding her baby boy.

Milly and another officer seem to be herding them towards the gate to Sand.

Jamileh pleads and begs. 'Please! No! Don't send us back! Please not Nauru!'

Shadi holds the baby tight. Refuses to keep walking.

Jamileh falls to the ground, clutching Milly's leg.

The crowd swells around them, pulsing with anger. Fear. Dismay.

Two more officers appear with another family, another baby, to be sent away. The father starts banging his head against the brick wall until his forehead is a mess of bloody flesh.

A skull of exploded red.

A curve of grey-white bone.

There is wailing and screaming all around us, as loud as sirens. A pregnant mother appears on the third-floor balcony, threatening to jump if she has to go. I see an officer sprint towards the stairs.

... blood-curdling screams ...

Nearby, two men climb onto the roof. Below, a furious mob faces off against the officers, throwing rubbish bins and yelling and smashing windows and shaking the fence and bashing on doors.

I search for Baba's face in the crowd.

The world is tear-stained.
I don't know what to do, where to run, what to think.

The air smells of sick and salt.

I can't see Arash. I scream his name.

Maman grabs Setareh from her pram and limps, as fast as she can, towards the compound fence.

It is almost like freedom ...

I yell, 'Maman! Stop! Wait!' But she's already trying to climb, clawing at the wire with one desperate hand; the other clutching Setareh against her chest.

I run towards her, begging her to stop.

An officer appears in front of me and peels Maman from the fence. It is Blockhead. He shoves her heavily to the ground.

The policemen yell at us, 'You sluts!'

Fear shrieks through every cell of my body as I keep running, desperate to help Maman, to hold Setareh.

A hand shoots out and grabs my hair.

My headscarf is ripped off and thrown to the ground.

... a fiery iron band ...

I twist and scream, arms flailing.

Blockhead yells something, his booming voice deafening in my ears.

My fingernails drag across rough, prickly skin, then my body is released.

For a moment I am free.

Then two hands grab me from behind, twisting my arms behind my back, dipping my face roughly towards the ground.

Something pointed and metal presses into my back.

My lips and chin scrape raw.

I feel the whip cut into the flesh on my back, again and again and again and again.

I taste blood and I can hear myself screaming, 'Maman! Maman!'

A man's voice yells out.

I thrash wildly, frantically, madly.

Security rushes to restrain ...

I see the guard holding me down.
It is Kenny.
My stomach lurches.
I rasp his name.
He takes hold of my wrist and pounds it into the concrete.

Crimson water gurgles as it swirls down the drain.

The crunch of breaking glass sounds like it's inside my head.

KENNY

Anger and fear and desperation pump through my veins. I can feel the girl's body shaking as I hold her down. My knee is in the small of her back, one hand on her wrist, the other hard on her bare neck. I wonder if I'm breaking some kind of Muslim law by touching her hair. I'm so close I can see bald patches and scabs amongst the waves of dark brown.

I look around and see her headscarf lying ripped nearby.

The concrete seems to glitter with minuscule shards of glass from the girl's watch. The watch Jonathan gave her. The watch I just smashed.

The girl is weeping and distraught, as she sobs for her mother.

Suddenly I let her go and stand up, the adrenaline finally subsiding as I look around. No-one pays me any attention; the whole centre is a chaos of screams and wails. I'm relieved to see that the riot police have arrived; they separate groups and herd bystanders into their rooms.

The girl looks up at me with hunted eyes. A shudder runs right through the core of me. What have I done?

The shift leader appears beside me. 'You alright?'

I nod but can't bring myself to speak.

Later, when I'm writing up the report, I run the incident through my mind again and again. The mother scrambling frantically at the fence, her movements ineffectual and lopsided. She couldn't use the arm that was holding the baby. Did Rick really have to shove her to the ground? And when the girl charged towards Rick. Was she angry? Or confused? Or scared? I remember Rick yelling, 'Grab her! Control and restraint!'

Is that what he did? Is that what *I* did? Controlled and restrained?

I can't be sure. The events are now soaked in the red of my fury, along with a sinking sense of guilt.

Were my actions a lapse of judgement? An overreaction? A fit of rage?

I can't think straight. The girl's screams are still shrill in my ears. I recall seeing the watch on her wrist. An image of Jonathan weeping in bed flashing into my mind. The dragon up on its haunches, bellowing clouds of fire. The smack of flesh on concrete, and the crunch of glass.

I remember someone here telling me, 'Whatever you do, don't admit fault.' I convince myself there's no point coming clean. If the operations manager finds out I used force on a minor, there'll be a formal investigation. They'll find out about Jonathan and the watch and who knows what else. I could be fired. And I can't afford to be out of work, especially now, with the news that Jonathan's been selling drugs.

I type 'control and restraint' into my report about the mother, but omit any mention of the girl. If she makes a complaint, or it was captured on the CCTV, I'll just say I forgot. It's a believable excuse; so much of the riot is already a blur.

There's a tap on my shoulder. I turn in my chair and see Rick sitting at the computer behind me.

'Did you hear me?' he says.

'Sorry. What?'

'I was saying I should charge that little bitch. Fucking scratched me. Look.'

There is a thin scrape of red amongst the stubble on his chin.

I start to panic. 'You can't put that in your report. Don't even mention her. She's a minor, remember?'

'Oh yeah. Fuck. Thanks.' He turns back to writing his up.

I do the same. I haven't even finished this report, and there are so many still to do. I realise I'd better call home.

Minh answers her mobile on the second ring. 'You interrupt my game. I'm playing *Candy Crush*. Jono show me.' She sounds bizarrely proud.

I tell her the centre is in lockdown. I don't know if the staff will be allowed out by 6.00am.

'I'm still hoping we are,' I say. 'But if I'm not home in time, can you please take Jonathan to school?'

JONO

I hear Aunty Minh talking to Dad in low, worried tones on her phone. She speaks in Vietnamese, so I can't understand, but her forehead is pinched with concern, and her words sound strained.

She hangs up and says, 'Your dad stuck at work.'

'What happened?' I ask.

'I can't say.'

I grab my laptop from my room.

It takes me two seconds to google: *Wickham Point today*.

An *NT News* article comes straight up. A picture of a high electric fence, with the headline: *Riot erupts at Wickham Point detention centre protesting moving family and pregnant woman to Nauru*.

I think of Ana. She wasn't at school today.

I quickly scan the piece. Aunty Minh comes to read over my shoulder.

... at least 20 detainees ...

... self-harming ...

... attempted suicide ...

... further abuse ...

My heart thuds loud with fear.

'Can we call Dad back and ask about my ... friend?'

Aunty Minh shakes her head.

'Or call the detention centre?'

'No way they tell you anything.'

I know she's right.

I send Ana a message, but am sickeningly sure she won't reply.

KENNY

I drive home exhausted. Eyelids heavy. A loud honk blasts me back to attention, as a bus of Inpex workers thunders past me in the opposite direction. I shake my head and take a large gulp of air. We're never allowed to sleep on night shift, but this was something else. Incidents kept flaring up, like spot fires that had to be put out. I was on my feet all night, running from one nightmare to the next. The only good thing about it was there wasn't too much time to think about the girl, or what I did, or what might happen if management finds out.

As I near home, I feel a growing sense of dread. I don't want to face Jonathan. But I've barely stopped the engine and opened the car door, when he appears.

'Dad. Is Ana alright? Is she still there? Did they deport her?'

'No.'

'Are they going to?'

'I don't know.' I'm too tired to ask how Jonathan knows what happened. I feel as if I'm returning from a war zone. I stagger towards the house. All I want is a shower. Clean clothes. My own bed.

But Jonathan won't let up. He buzzes around me like a persistent fly.

'Will she be at school today?'

'There's no way the bus will run.'

'I want to go and see her.'

'The place is in semi-lockdown. No visitors allowed.'

'Well, when they're allowed again –'

'You're grounded, remember?'

'I don't care. Take me or I'll find a way to go alone.'

'You can't. You need an adult.' I pray that's a knockout blow.

I can still see the fear in the girl's eyes. Hear the terrified pitch of her screams.

I start to drag my tired body down the hall, then stop when I hear Minh say, 'I take you.'

'What?' I wheel around. 'You can't do that! I won't let you! You're supposed to be on my side!'

Minh stands her ground, hands on hips. 'There are no sides, Dzoung. That place is warping your brain.'

Jonathan scrambles to get his laptop from the kitchen bench. He clicks at the mousepad and a Word document fills the screen. A visit-request form.

'Where did you get that from?'

'I called up ages ago. But I need her boat number. Do you know it?'

I think about saying no, but even pleading ignorance will only buy me so much time. Jonathan will find out from the girl or someone else. It hits me like a tidal wave: Jonathan will find out what I've done. Sooner or later, he'll know. And, when he does, he's going to hate me even more than he already does.

It all seems inevitable.

I surrender. Feel my body go limp.

'It's KIN016,' I say. 'But you'll need the numbers for her mum and siblings too. Here, give me the laptop.'

Jonathan watches as I type the numbers into the form.

KIN016

KIN015
KIN014
KIN014.1

ANA

We can't find out what's happening.

No one knows.

Jamileh and Shadi and the baby are still here in Surf.

Zahra and I go to see her, but she doesn't say much.

They're under high watch; an officer stands listening to our Farsi with suspicious eyes.

The pregnant mother who threatened to jump is being monitored too.

She stands, holding her belly, staring vacantly into the courtyard.

Maman barely moves from her mattress on the floor.

I take Arash and Setareh to the playground, and the common room, and the Mess.

Wherever we go, the air is thick with terrified speculation about who will be sent to Nauru, and how and when they'll go.

Days blur into nights and lighten into day again.

One morning, one of the Mohammeds wanders past me in school uniform.

I realise he is going to catch the bus.

School seems like a distant dream.

Jono does too.

Every day I fill out request forms to see Eliza.

I write long heartfelt pleas in carefully printed English, using words from the dictionary like 'survive' and 'cruel'.

But the days pass, and Eliza doesn't come.

Where is she? I wonder. What is she doing when she's not here?

Meena tries to reassure Maman, saying Eliza probably has a family to look after.

But I know that, in Australia, Eliza is young.

I imagine her out doing the things Jono has described.

Like eating thin pancakes with liquid chocolate and strawberries at the markets.

Or dancing at an outdoor concert, drinking beer.

I try putting pictures in the requests and complaints box, along with the usual form.

They are drawings by Arash.

Stick figures behind thick black bars.

One of them shows a scribble of a child standing next to a green-crayon coffin.

I use simple words on the form now, remembering her tears and hoping they can save us.

I write: *Eliza. Please come. Please help.*

JONO

School starts again, but lunchtimes are empty without Ana. I return to the outer. Mel gives me a punch on the arm and jokes, 'Our prodigal friend.' Mac and Ibrahim welcome me back into the *Candy Crush* fold with open arms. Will is happy, but senses my return is reluctant, and potentially short-lived.

My first request to see Ana is declined: visits take a few days to start again after the riot. They knock back my second request too: the day we chose is already full. I change the date and submit the form again.

I wait for the detention centre bus in the mornings. Kids start to trickle back, but neither Zahra nor Ana reappears.

I send more messages via Facebook, but Ana doesn't reply.

Dad is back on day shifts. He still has my borrowed phone, but at least he hasn't returned it or talked to Will's mum about the pot. He's determined to limit our contact though, and keeps me under surveillance. Won't even let me skate to school. So Aunty Minh comes in the mornings, and dinks me there on her motorbike. In the afternoons, she picks me up and stays at our house till Dad returns. Or, some days, we go to her tiny flat instead.

I pretend to do homework on her old desktop computer as I watch her potter around. She seems to magically know where everything is, despite the leaning towers of junk. I could swear everything she owns is piled up on the floor. She doesn't have much furniture; it must be the one thing she doesn't hoard. The walls are empty, except for a framed copy of her citizenship certificate, proudly displayed behind the TV.

Today, she burrows in a corner, shoving heavy stacks of old mail and a toaster to one side. She emerges with a victorious grin and a tarnished metal spoon. 'This! This is what I want to show you, Jonathan.'

I don't hate my name quite as much the way she pronounces it. *Jon-o-tun.*

She says, 'This is the spoon they give me when I first arrive. You remember I tell you? About the boat? This spoon is from St Vincent de Paul. Very nice people. Make me feel very welcome. Very happy and warm.' She places it on the desk, next to the monitor. 'You. You have it now.'

I laugh. 'Thanks. Just what I always wanted, Cô Minh.'

She grins back at me, with yellowing teeth. 'You always cheeky. Cheeky boy.'

I turn back to the computer and check my inbox. There's a new email from Raj, the guy who organises the visits at Wickham Point. I've emailed so many times now that I know him by name.

I open it up. And, finally, there it is.

I tell Aunty Minh: 'They say we can visit on Friday. That's still okay for you, right?'

She nods. 'Yes. Friday we will go.'

ANA

My reflection swims in the steel mirror.
More patches of blood,
and missing clumps of hair.
I tell Zahra I want to shave it off.
Worry creases her brow. 'Are you sure?'
I say, 'Yes.'
'The officer who cuts hair is really bad.'

'You do it then.'
She reluctantly agrees.
Neither of us mentions Jono,
or school.
Arash watches silently from the corner.
The officer-who-cuts-hair folds her arms and frowns.
The razor buzzes against my skull
In careful, deliberate lines.
Long locks of brown
hit the floor.

KENNY

I argue with Minh over dinner, speaking in Vietnamese so Jonathan can't understand.

'Why are you doing this?' I ask. 'Why are you taking him in there?'

Minh stares straight back at me. 'Why don't you want him to go? Because he might see the *hotel*? Because maybe you feel ashamed of where you work?'

'I'm not ashamed of my job. I need to earn money. It pays.'

'Then let Jonathan see his girlfriend.'

'He shouldn't even have a girlfriend. He's too young. You know how emotional he gets.'

'He's not the only one.'

My breathing is laboured. There's a pain in my chest.

'Are you working on Friday?' asks Minh.

I tell her I have the day off.

'We'll need to borrow your car. My motorbike might not make it all the way out there.' I hesitate, wondering if I can put an end to the idea of them visiting by refusing the use of my car. But then she adds, 'Or, if you won't lend it to us, I can always ask Phoung. Of course, I'd have to tell her you were too stingy to let us take yours.'

I glare at her. 'Fine. Take the car.'

ANA

Zahra hands me
a rectangle strip of white paper
she snuck out from the Mess.
It's a visit-request slip
for me, Maman, Arash and Setareh.
From Minh and Jonathan Do.
For 3.15pm tomorrow afternoon.
I say, 'I can't.'
I can still feel the imprint
of Kenny's hands on my neck.
There's pity in Zahra's eyes.
'I understand why this is hard.
But I need you to go. I need your help.'
She holds out a tiny SIM card in her palm.
'Please, Ana. I have fifty photos on here.
If he can just give it to the newspaper.'
I look from Setareh spluttering in my arms,
to Arash watching cartoons,

and Maman sleeping on the floor.
'Even if I went ... how would I explain it to Maman?'
'Just say ... he's a tutor. From the school.'
'I can't. I'm sorry. I just can't ask him.
Not after what his dad did.'
'Are you kidding?
Especially after what his dad did.
He'll probably beg you to let him help
to make it up to you.'
I hesitate. 'I thought you said he was a Soc
and he'd never understand.'
She holds the SIM card out again.
'Socs don't bring food to movies in plastic bags.'

KENNY

I wait for the familiar 'Yeah?' then enter Jonathan's room. I brace myself for attitude, but there is no slouch or snarl. I place the iPhone he borrowed from Will on the side of his desk, hoping he understands that returning it is my way of raising a white flag. He nods acknowledgement, as I sit hesitantly on the end of his single bed. The faded *Star Wars* doona reminds me of Roxanne; the thought of her is a punch in the guts.

'I should buy you a new doona cover,' I say. 'Maybe for Christmas.'

'Sure. That'd be good.'

The space between us feels cavernous. I need to reach

him. Protect him. Protect myself. I can't let him get any more entangled in this than he already is.

'Jono …' The shortened name feels strange on my lips. 'I know you're going to visit that girl tomorrow and –'

'Her name's Anahita.'

'Yes.' I try again. 'I know you're going to visit her – Anahita – and I just wanted to say … Please, be careful.'

'Dad –'

'If she asks you for anything else – or for help – just say no.'

I'm careful not to bring up the drug dealing or him being grounded. I can't afford any bad will between us. Especially now, after what I've done.

'She's never asked me for anything,' he says. 'The movies and the watch were my idea. And she didn't know anything about the pot or anything else.'

I take this in. 'Okay, but if she asks you –'

'She won't –'

'Please. Just listen. The detainees … they're desperate at the moment. People are being moved. And there's nothing you or I can do about that. It's just how the system works.'

'Are they going to move her?'

'I have no idea. All I know is people who come here like that – by boat – they come praying for a better life. And I understand that. I really do. I had to wait three years before my visa was approved. Three years of Minh trying to sponsor me and me chasing documents and waiting in Vietnam. My life could've been different if I'd been able to come when I was eighteen, not twenty-one. But I waited. And I got here legally. These people don't do that. They don't wait. They pay money and they come. Many of them aren't even real refugees, but they do and say whatever they need to in order to be allowed to stay.'

'I know Ana. She's not like that.'

'Maybe not. But ... whatever she tells you, take it with a grain of salt.' I feel the tug of guilt, but kick it away. My relationship with Jonathan has to come first. The girl will be gone soon, but our bond is for life.

Jonathan frowns, but says, 'Alright.'

Relief rushes through my body. I stand and impulsively ruffle his hair, like I used to when he was small.

Emotion wells up inside me, as I say, 'I know it might not always seem like it, but everything I do, I do because I care.'

Jonathan looks up and meets my eye. 'I do know that, Dad. I know.'

JONO

I stare out the passenger window as Aunty Minh drives out of the city. She insists on playing the Vietnamese elevator music Dad keeps in the car. We head out past Palmerston, into the bush. It feels like it's taking forever. The music doesn't help. But when I check the clock it has only been half an hour.

'How much further?' I ask.

'Ten minute.'

'Why do they keep them so far away?'

Aunty Minh shrugs. 'It not even illegal, you know. Come by boat.'

We fall quiet again. Eventually, I see a sign to Wickham Point on the side of the road.

Aunty Minh turns left into a driveway curtained by manicured grass, planted trees and carefully positioned landscaping rocks. She pulls up at a boom gate. An Indian guard wearing a turban emerges from a small hut. I wonder if it is Raj.

He approaches the driver's side. Aunty Minh winds her window down. 'Hello. We here for visit?'

'Got your licence?'

She hands it to him, and he takes it back to the hut. A few moments later he reappears and hands it back. 'You know where to go?'

'I know,' says Aunty Minh.

He steps aside, and the boom gate opens. We drive slowly forwards, then find a park and climb out.

The full metal horror of the detention centre rears up in front of me. Fence after fence after fence. I recognise the outermost one from the photo in the *NT News*: it is topped with thin lines, rows of electric wires. There are security cameras too. And holding yards. And concrete. So much concrete. Everything reinforced, built to contain and confine.

'Come on.' Aunty Minh beckons me forwards.

I follow her numbly down a path to a small demountable office. Mosquitoes whine around my ears; I slap them away.

Inside, another guard asks for ID. Aunty Minh shows her licence again. I hand him my student card. He writes something in a logbook, then hands us dog tags to put around our necks.

The front says *VISITOR*. I flip it over. On the back is a list entitled: *Colour Emergency Response Codes.* Red is fire. Orange is evacuation. Purple is bomb threat. Grey is major disturbance.

I wonder if the riot was Grey.

The guard hands Aunty Minh a key, and nods towards a bank of lockers behind us. 'Just pop your stuff in there – all bags, phones, identification. You can't take any of that stuff in.'

'But … we brought a few things. For the person we're going to visit,' I say.

'Only food allowed.'

'What about these?' I hold out a pair of shoelaces covered in rows of koalas. I found them in the two-dollar shop in Nightcliff and thought they'd make Ana smile. But the guard holds them up and shakes his head. 'Sorry, mate. People have hung themselves with less than this.' My eyes widen in horror. The guard laughs. 'Sorry, sorry. Bad joke. You can give them to your friend, you just can't take them in. I'll sign them into property and they can pick them up later.'

I sign the form and push the laces across the desk. I wonder if she'll really get them, or if this is another bad joke.

Aunty Minh holds up a plastic container of sliced watermelon, picked fresh from our garden at home. 'What about this? This good?'

The guard seems to waver. 'You're only really supposed to take in packaged food. But I guess it's alright.'

Aunty Minh places it on the conveyor belt. It goes through a machine like the ones that scan bags at the airport. We walk through the human-sized version, and grab the watermelon on the other side.

The guard unlocks the door, pushes it open and points. 'See that little place there? That's the visitors' building. Just follow the path.'

ANA

I walk the fence,
like hundreds of feet before me.
And probably after too.
There is a thin track worn into the red-brown dirt.
I carry Setareh in my arms,
Praying that her little footprints never join mine in here.
The big clock on the wall outside the Mess says
ten past three.
I stop mid-lap, by the officer at the gate.
'Excuse me. I have visit request …
But my Maman is sick.
Can I go without her?'
He examines the slip,
then asks, 'Is KIN015 an adult?'
'No. Is my little brother.'
'You need at least one adult.'
I think of Meena and ask, 'Can it be someone else?'
His tone is final. 'Sorry, sweetheart.
Just whoever's listed on there.'

JONO

There is metal all around us now. Fences everywhere I look. Blocking off buildings. Cross-hatching the hills. Scarring the sky.

My mind is a mess of questions. Is this really where Ana's been living all this time? Why didn't she tell me how horrible it is? Or is it possible that I didn't listen when she tried?

We enter the visitors' room. It is small and clean but impersonal, with a row of plastic tables and chairs. There's a sink and bar fridge at the far end, and in front of us is a low black vinyl couch occupied by a family with a baby and a little girl. They're being visited by a woman who has the glow of the church about her. A guard watches from a high, narrow desk nearby.

Beyond them, out the back doorway, I see another fence, then a small hill of red earth and gum trees, just out of reach.

Aunty Minh takes a seat at one of the tables. I sit in a chair beside her; the plastic legs bend and bow under my weight.

'You tell her, right? You say we are coming?' asks Aunty Minh.

I nod.

'Sometime they don't get message. My friends tell me,' she says.

'I told her on Facebook.'

'Ah. Good.'

I don't tell her that Ana didn't reply. She hasn't answered anything I've sent, hasn't even been online, or at least not that I've seen. And I've checked a lot.

Nerves gnaw at my insides.

Aunty Minh settles back in her chair, more confident than I feel. 'We wait. She come.'

ANA

Urgent steps
back to our room.
Door squeaks open.
Arash looks up from the TV.
Maman's eyes are open, but she hasn't moved.
I touch her shoulder, light as the gentle breeze outside.
'Maman?'
She blinks, but doesn't reply.

JONO

I fidget on the chair, scratching at the mosquito bites already swelling red against my skin. No wonder Ana is always covered in them. I remember joining the ones on her arm in pen one lunchtime, in a funny kind of dot to dot. Her laughter was sudden and beautiful, like a wet season downpour of rain.

The red hand of the clock on the wall inches around to 3.25pm.

'Maybe we should go,' I say.

Aunty Minh walks up to the guard at the high desk.

'You know if they coming?'

He shrugs, slow and laconic. 'Dunno. They've been told. But sometimes they just don't show up.' As an afterthought, he adds, 'Sorry.'

Aunty Minh turns back to me. 'Maybe we try again another day.'

I stand, picking up the plastic container of watermelon, and turn towards the door … and there she is. A tiny baby in her arms.

An old woman by her side. A little boy clinging to her leg.

It throws me, this strange new family context. But it's her. It's definitely her.

I say, 'Ana', and take a step forwards. I want to hold her, kiss her, make sure she's alright.

But as if she reads my mind, she whispers in English: 'No … cuddle.' I wonder if she looked that word up in the dictionary just before she came. 'We are not allowed. Only one short … cuddle … at start and end. But please don't. Maman would not understand.'

I look around for her mother, then realise she must be talking about the old lady. I nod towards her. 'That's your mum?'

'Yes,' Ana says.

I introduce Aunty Minh, who coos, 'How old the baby?'

I've never heard her voice so gooey and soft.

In contrast, Ana seems as if every word pains her. 'Almost three month.'

'Wah … so small. I hold her?'

Ana nods, and Aunty Minh takes the baby gently, so gently, into her arms. She nods to Ana's mother. 'We sit outside?'

They move to the door. There are metal tables out there, with chairs bolted to the ground. The two women take a seat. Aunty Minh presses her nose to the baby's head and inhales deeply, like it is the best perfume in the world.

I look around for the little brother, but he's run off to play with the little girl from the family on the couch.

Ana and I are suddenly alone.

I sit clumsily back down on the plastic chair. Ana sits on Aunty Minh's.

She looks worriedly out at her mother. 'Her English not so good.'

'My aunty's isn't either – and she's been here forever.'

We share a small smile.

I notice there's a graze on her lips, her chin. 'What happened?' I ask.

She frowns, touching her lips. 'Oh. I hurt ...'

I wait for her to continue, but she doesn't say any more. I wonder if it is from the riot. Was she involved?

I take a piece of watermelon, and hold the container out towards her, but she declines. Her movements are stiff and strange.

'I hope you don't mind me coming,' I say. 'I know you said not to ... but with the riot ... and you not at school ... I was worried. I sent you messages.'

'I did not have time for computer.'

'Right.'

I study her, trying to figure out what's changed. She's not in school uniform, of course. And she's wearing a headscarf that I've never seen. It's tied differently too.

I realise I can't see the usual arc of brown hair near her

forehead. 'Your scarf ... did you cut your hair?'

'Yes. It was ... hot.' She seems uneasy.

I try to pretend we're in the hallway at school, rather than a fenced and guarded room. I say, 'But it's going to cool down soon, remember? Dry season's almost here. Did you notice the dragonflies? That's always a sure sign the weather's starting to change.'

I take in the drawn look of her cheeks, the rigid set of her shoulders, the thinness of her arms.

My gaze stops at her wrist. 'Where's the watch?'

'Sorry?'

'The watch I gave you.'

Her body seems to contract, and she won't meet my eyes. I think of what Dad said about the black market.

'Did you sell it?'

'No.'

'It's okay if you did.'

She pulls back, almost haughty, like I've insulted her. 'I did not.'

There's another awkward silence. Ana looks conflicted, almost tortured. I'm confused. I look outside again. Aunty Minh is sitting there with Ana's mother, side by side. They're not talking, but Ana's mum's posture tells me she finds my aunty's presence soothing. There's something unspoken and beautiful about it, and I feel a burst of pride.

I turn back to Ana and the words start to pour out of me. 'I've missed you.'

'Jono ... I need help.'

Everything around us fades. I feel like vomiting.

She lowers her voice to a whisper. 'I am scared ... scared

they send us back to Nauru … there is … black mark on my file … the cinema … your dad … riot …'

Her grasp of English seems to be disintegrating with every word. I barely know her, this stumbling, desperate version of Ana.

She pulls something from her pocket, and holds it in her fingers, just below the table. 'I don't want ask … but if you can take this … it is photos … babies, children … if you can give to news …' She breaks off. Her watery eyes plead for understanding. 'I do not like ask. I would not ask. But I am … at zero …'

I can barely hear her above the roar of Dad's warnings in my head.

… she will ask for help …

… they do and say whatever they need to in order to be allowed to stay …

My eyes fall on her wrist again. 'Tell me the truth about the watch. Did you sell it?'

Her hands hover above her lap, then fall onto her knees. She still won't meet my eyes. 'No. In riot … your dad … pull hair … break watch … hurt me …'

I look at the graze on her lips.

I think of all the times Dad's yelled at me. All the times fury's burnt in his eyes.

But he's never touched me.

Never hit me.

Not once.

I feel his hand clapped proudly on my back. See the smile in his eyes.

… everything I do, I do because I care …

I push my chair back. The plastic legs scrape loudly on the floor.

'No. He wouldn't,' I say.

She frowns, as if she's trying to make sense of my words.

I repeat myself, louder this time. And surer. 'He wouldn't do that.'

She stares at me, disbelieving. I stare straight back.

The space between us feels huge and gaping.

I think of her mum and her brother and the baby. She's never talked much about them, or what it's like in here. I think of her newly cut hair, and the SIM card in her palm. The allegation of the smashed watch and Dad's abuse.

There is so much she hasn't told me. So much that I don't know.

... many of them aren't even real refugees ...

I hear my voice, echoey and harsh. 'Why did you leave Iran?'

Every fibre of her body seems to freeze. 'What?'

'You never told me. Why did you leave?'

I see her eyes close down. Give up. Shut me out.

She stands abruptly, voice cracking as she says, 'Go. Please. Do not come again.'

Then she's moving towards the back door, saying something to her mother in Farsi, and prising the baby from my aunty's arms.

Aunty Minh looks stunned. Her grip is tight, like she doesn't want to let it go. I realise her face is covered in tears.

Ana calls to her little brother and starts towards the exit, the baby in one arm, and her mother supported with the other.

'Ana ...' I call.

The guard moves out from behind his desk, like he's worried he might have to intervene.

The brother scampers to Ana's side. Her headscarf loosens, and I think I see a gleam of bare shaved scalp.

Then she's out the door.

And I just stand there.

ANA

I walk to the gate,
carrying
my heart
in my hands.
Can't anyone see it,
haemorrhaging
in my palms?
Can't they see
the blood
trailing me
on the ground?

JONO

I feel a tap on my shoulder.

'Hey ... everything alright?' It's the guy from behind the desk. His eyes are kind. 'By the way, you're supposed to be wearing closed shoes,' he says. 'I didn't want to tell you until the end of your visit 'cause then I couldn't let you stay. But, just so you know, for next time.'

I manage to nod.

I hear Aunty Minh say, 'Thank you.'

We walk out of the visitors' room, back to the demountable, and wait to be buzzed out.

The door clicks locked behind us as we leave.

ANA

At the third gate,
Maman mumbles,
'Who was that Chinese lady?
And the boy?'
Her eyes are glassy.
I am alone.
I don't even bother
making an excuse.
I say, 'No-one, Maman.'
She doesn't ask again.

JONO

Aunty Minh waits until she's settled into the driver's seat, before she asks, 'What happen?'

I can't bring myself to reply. If I do, I might start crying, and she'll tell Dad, and he'll take it as further confirmation that I'm weak. A small flare of anger ignites in my chest. What does Dad really know about me, anyway? What does Dad know about anything?

He was right about Ana asking me for help, but ... But what?

My mind sifts back through time, making an inventory of things that don't add up.

The way Dad could barely meet my gaze last night.

The fact he called me Jono.

The smell of smoke on his breath.

The glimpse of Ana's shaved scalp.

The pain in her eyes when I asked why she left Iran.

'You want to talk about it?' asks Aunty Minh.

'Do you?' I turn the question back on her. 'Why were you crying?'

She shakes her head.

We drive in silence the whole way home.

ANA

Zahra is waiting
outside our room.
She sees my face,
and doesn't ask.
Her eyes are teary,
as I put the SIM card
back into her hand.

KENNY

I know something is wrong as soon as they arrive home. I hang back to talk to Minh, as Jonathan storms past me into the house.

'What happened?' Dread floods my body, as I imagine the worst. *She told him I abused her. I pretty much did. He'll never talk to me again. And I deserve it.*

'I think she break up with him,' says Minh.

'What?' I stare at her.

'I think ...' Minh clenches her fists in front of her and rotates them, as if snapping something invisible in her hands.

Jonathan bursts back out of his room. He walks right up to me, so close that I could swear I smell watermelon on his breath.

'You hit her.' There's conviction in his voice.

I meet his hard gaze straight on, and know there's no point denying it. 'I was just ... doing my job ...'

He explodes. 'How can you even work out there? It's a fucking jail! A jail for people who've done nothing wrong except come here by boat. It's not even fucking illegal – did you know that? Aunty Minh told me.'

I flash a look at Minh, but she just shrugs. 'It not secret, Dzoung. It the law.'

Jonathan is crying now. He glowers at me, but doesn't falter or wipe the tears away.

Instead, he says, 'You think I'm pathetic and weak, but you know what? At least I'm not a fucking unemotional robot like you. You have no heart. No wonder Mum left you.'

His words hit me like physical blows. I feel myself gasping for air.

JONO

And then I'm running. I don't know where or why or how. All I know is I can't stay there at home with him. My muscles kick automatically into gear. Houses blur into streets into shops into trees into parks.

I double over and dry-retch.

A girl with pigtails watches from a nearby playground. Her mother shepherds her away.

I slump, my chest heaving in and out with every breath. I'm still angry at Dad, but I'm more angry at myself. It wasn't his fault. It was mine.

I didn't trust Ana.

I let her down.

I hear her voice. *Do not come again.*

Shadows stretch across grass onto bitumen road.

I pull my dumbphone out of my pocket and call Will. 'Let's get smashed.'

We go back to the Ludshed. It's been weeks since I was last there. I shove the door open to see that the inside has been totally trashed. There's graffiti everywhere: tags, mostly. Blackened walls, like they've lit fires. One corner is burnt out and littered with smashed bottles.

'Recycling,' a random Year 11 tells me, laughing.

In another corner someone's dragged in a threadbare armchair. It's covered in slashes of red spray paint. Someone is playing heavy metal from a portable speaker. The sound is crap, bouncing back at us from the corrugated iron walls.

I don't recognise anyone from last time, but I don't care.

Will lights up and starts to pass doobies around. I help him start a mini-production line. One of my hands is permanently rolling, the other smoking or drinking or swallowing whatever is put in it.

The older guys treat us like celebrities. I don't kid myself; I know it's because of the pot, which Will is handing out with abandon, often forgetting to take money in return. He seems almost manic, laughing and grinning in my face, like he thinks fun and nonstop action will keep my tears at bay. I understand that he's scared of me sinking again.

I am too.

We smoke and drink and laugh and get high until the

world is blurry and the pain is numb.

But even in the haze, she is there, watching me with hurt reproach.

ANA

My voice is small.
I say, 'Maman?
I want to go back to Iran.'
I think of Baba's old saying,
about running from a snake
only to end up in a dragon's mouth.
For a long time, Maman is quiet.
Then I hear her say,
'We can't.'

KENNY

I sit alone on the old velvet couch in the lounge room. The sky outside is dark. Minh left hours ago, patting my shoulder goodbye with disappointment in her eyes.

'You need to find a new job.'

I didn't argue or disagree. I think about calling her now, but don't have anything new to report. Jonathan's still not answering his phone, and Will's mum had no idea where they could be.

He could be anywhere.

All I ever wanted was to protect him.

And now he's out there, doing God knows what ... and all I can do is sit here ... helpless and completely alone ...

A sob wrenches itself from my gut into my mouth. I gurgle in shock. Try to push it back down. But then another comes. And another. Wave upon wave upon wave.

I sob noisily. Messily. Uncontrollably.

ANA

I close my eyes.
Shadows of nightmares
swim into view.
Smooth tan hands.
Thin, angular body.
Triangle eyes.
Unkind.
I wake in a tangle
of wet sheets
and incoherent screams.
Arash stares at me
with panicked eyes.
'Ana? I wet the bed again.'
He starts to cry.
I change the bedding,
then settle him back to sleep.
Maman doesn't stir.

I pull her
bottle of black market
sleeping pills
from where they're hidden
in the cupboard
and swallow one.
Then another.
And another.
I'm ...

JONO

... on the floor.

One of the boys is smashing up the toilets with an axe. A couple is kissing, their bodies crushed together in the tiny armchair. Some guy is passed out beside me, slumped and drooling onto the filthy, charred concrete.

A male voice says, 'Hey, Nippy. Smoke?' Something in its tone rubs the wrong way. It sounds bossy. Ungrateful. Rude.

'Don't call me that,' I say.

'What?'

I look up and see the random Year 11 from earlier. 'Don't call me Nippy. Only mates ...' I'm slurring but I don't care.

The guy rolls his eyes. 'Whatever, *mate*. Give us a smoke.' He holds out an empty palm.

And suddenly I'm lurching to my feet, fists swinging. I can hear guys hollering and cheering, and my feet are flying and my fist impacts. Then his does. One, two, three. He's better than me. I taste blood. It tastes good. Salty. Bitter. Alive.

I stagger forwards, cliches streaming from my mouth.

'You want a piece of me?'

'Think you're fucking good?'

'Hit me again.'

And then I'm on top of him, slamming his head back into the ground. Is this what Dad did to Ana?

I hear the thud of skull on concrete, then someone seizes me from behind.

'Jono. Jono. Stop! Get off him!' It's Will. 'I'm serious, man. Fucking run. There's police.'

I scramble backwards, vision reeling, and catch sight of two cops in the corner with a bony Aboriginal man. He's pointing around the shed, hand swinging wildly. I hear him say: ' They nicked my generator ... been trespassing ...'

Everyone is bolting now. Clambering out the windows. Sprinting out the doors.

I move to follow them, but a blur of blue hoists me back, marches me outside to a paddy wagon and shoves me in. There's a bunch of people already inside. Will is thrown in after me.

The policeman locks the door.

And then we're driving.

The cool night air streams into our little cell.

Darwin flashes past, framed by the square grids of our wire cage.

And then I ...

ANA

... black out.
Someone shakes my shoulders.
A woman's voice,
garbled and strange.
'Get up.'
I'm underwater.
My eyes are glue,
and my body is heavy.
'Come on. Get up. You're being moved.'
Hands under arms.
Feet on cool tiles.
I sway.
Someone's body against mine.
'Shit! Come on! Wake up! Stand up! Start walking!'
Hands yanked behind my back,
pinned to my waist.
I urge my eyes open,
see the orange rug on the floor,
remember promising it to Zahra:
how will I get it to her now?
Try to form my lips
around the words:
'Our things ...'
A shake of red curls.
Milly.
Her tone is cold.
'Leave your stuff.
We'll pack it up.

And get any items from property too.'
I'm pushed forwards,
head jerks back,
eyes up.
Pale star stickers,
barely visible in the
glaring fluorescent light.
I open my mouth,
but a hand clamps over it
and my bare head is wedged under
someone's arm.
They drag me out ...

JONO

... and line us up. Search our bodies for ID. A male cop pulls out what's left of Will's pot stash along with his wallet. He looks at the student ID and gives a low whistle. 'This one's Anthony Miller's son.'

'Who?' The female cop looks at him blankly.

'Big shot lawyer. Better call him straight away.' He turns to me. 'What about you, son? Who's your dad? Someone famous too?'

I slur my response. 'Nah. He's just an arsehole. A fucking no-one.'

He searches me anyway; I'm not carrying a wallet. I've only got my dumbphone on me; he tosses it dismissively to the female officer, then shouts in my face. 'What's your name?'

For no good reason, I say, 'Mohammed.'

Will cracks up laughing.

The policeman looks unimpressed. 'Got a last name, Mohammed?'

'Sorry.'

The Year 11 guy I punched speaks up from down the line. He glares at me, with one swollen eye and a bloody nose. 'He's full of shit. His friends call him Nippy.'

Will laughs even harder. 'Nippy! Does that sound like a real name to you?'

And then I'm cracking up too.

'You fucking Nip!' Will gasps.

And we're on the floor of the police station. Rolling, hysterical, crying, laughing.

I hear one of the cops say, 'Oh boy.'

KENNY

I feel the soft weight of my mobile in my hand. I press 'R' then select Roxanne's name. It rings. I think it's going to click onto voicemail, but suddenly she's there.

Her voice is sleepy but familiar. Comforting, even. 'Dzoung, is everything alright?' She always refused to call me Kenny.

'Yeah,' I say.

The flood of memories is so strong it almost washes me away. Roxanne riding the kids to school. Roxanne serving dinner at the outside table, asking about everyone's favourite things of the day. Roxanne in the garden, binoculars in her hands.

Her voice interrupts the deluge of images. 'Is there a reason why you're ringing?'

'Jonathan – has he called you?'

'I haven't spoken to him in ages.' There's accusation in her voice. 'Did something happen?'

I don't know where to begin.

Roxanne prompts: 'Lara said you think he has a girlfriend. Did that … go wrong?'

I know without asking that she is thinking about before, when Priya broke up with Jonathan and he got so depressed, so violently low. I know Roxanne blames herself for that; it happened just after she left.

I hurry to say, 'No, no, nothing like that. I mean, not really …' I have to force myself to continue. 'We had a fight. I really stuffed up. He ran out. And now I don't know where he is.'

I steel myself for her scorn, her condescension, her distaste. I want it. I deserve it.

But when Roxanne speaks again, her voice is soft. 'Hey … hey … it'll be alright. Whatever happened, it's okay. He has to come home eventually … and when he does, just say you're sorry, okay? And, in the meantime, I'll try to call him too. I'll use Lara's phone. He never answers when I call.' She pauses, then says, 'Why did you have to do that, Dzoung? Make him on your side?'

I am silent. Numb.

I choke out the words. 'I'm sorry.'

She's quick to say, 'It's okay. Forget I said that. It's alright.

I'll try him now and call you back.' She hangs up.

I recognise her words and actions for what they are: a grain of parental solidarity.

A kernel of forgiveness lying on the earth between us.

ANA

Stark white
brick box.
Maman rocking
on the floor.
River of Farsi,
and the repeated phrase:
'No Nauru ... please, no Nauru ...'
Eyes swing wildly
around the room.
A male officer bounces Setareh
in his arms.
I am grateful
that she is sleeping,
that this won't be imprinted
on her baby brain.
Another family,
another mother begging:
'Where are they taking us?
Please.
Can't you tell us anything?'
Milly shakes her head.

'Won't be much longer.'

But it is.

We wait.

And wait.

And wait.

And ...

JONO

... wake with a pounding head and sunlight striped across my face. Where the hell am I? The memories tumble in fast and backwards. *The police station. The cops. The fight. Will. Dad.*

Ana.

It hits me like a physical pain in the chest.

I close my eyes again.

Somewhere down the corridor I hear Will's voice. 'Can we take Jono home too?'

'Don't push your luck, buddy.' A gruff male, probably Will's dad.

Then a female, apologetic: 'It has to be a legal guardian in any case, as I'm sure you're aware, Mr Miller.' And then softer. 'Don't worry, your friend's dad's on the way.'

Will's dad again: 'Thanks, officer. Sorry for the trouble. And thanks again for not pressing charges.'

The door to the cop-shop screeches open then shut, accompanied by the light ring of a bell.

Then silence.

I lie there, numb and alone.

I wonder if this is what it's like for her in Wickham Point. Is Ana's room bigger or smaller than this? Do they lock the doors? Do the guards feel like police? There is so much I never dared to ask. So much I assumed but don't actually know.

The air inside my cell is thick with alcohol fumes and regret.

Eventually, I hear the sound I've been dreading: Dad's voice. Two sets of footsteps approach, and there's the clink of keys in the lock. 'Here he is. All yours.'

The door swings open. I can't look at him; I keep my eyes on the ground as he walks me out. We stop at the desk to sign some paperwork and reclaim my phone.

'Are there going to be any charges?' asks Dad.

'Not sure yet,' says the officer. 'We'll let you know.'

I think about arguing. I know Will's getting off and I wasn't even carrying pot. But Dad's look silences me. I follow him out to the car. He climbs into the driver's seat, then leans over to unlock the passenger door for me. I climb in and flick my phone open. There are nine missed calls from Lara.

I dial voicemail and wait to hear her voice. But instead I hear Mum. The gentle care in her voice throws me backwards through the years.

'Jono ... you there, darling? I know you don't want to talk to me ... but your dad's really worried ... he doesn't know where you are ... if you could just call him ...'

I hang up mid-message and look across at Dad. He's just sitting there in the driver's seat, holding the keys in his hand.

'It was Mum,' I say. 'How did she know?'

'I called her.'

'What?' I wonder how long it's been since they talked.

He repeats: 'I called your mother. Last night. I didn't know what else to do, who else would understand.' His voice wavers with emotion.

I don't move. I hardly breathe.

'She's not a bad person, you know. I'm sorry if I made you think she was. We're just ... different. It was what drew me to her at the start. She was always so carefree. With that smile. And those legs.' I squirm, but he doesn't seem to notice. 'And that hair. So blonde. My Australian girlfriend.'

I feel almost embarrassed for him. 'You say it like that's some kind of prize.'

'At the time it kind of felt like it was. I tried my best to be Australian too. Dropped out of engineering. Worked in construction. Wore stubbies and drank beer. Changed my name. Your mum hated it, always insisted on calling me Dzoung. We started fighting more and more. But by then we had Lara and you. She wanted me to teach you Vietnamese, but I didn't see the point.'

'I wish you had,' I say. And I mean it.

'Me too.' He looks me straight in the eyes. 'Wish I'd done a lot of things differently.'

And I know he is talking about Ana, and his job, and calling me pathetic and weak.

'I just want you to have the freedom to do something you love. Your mother does too. She offered to have you live with her actually, when Lara moved down at the start of this year.'

I stare at him.

'I know, I should've said … I'll understand if you want to move down there now.' He looks at me with fearful, searching eyes.

It is so much to take in.

'I don't know, Dad,' I say.

'Sure.' He seems to slump. 'Think about it. Take your time.'

He finally puts the keys in the ignition. The engine coughs into life then splutters out.

Dad turns and sees my incredulous expression. A smile creeps slowly across his face. 'Fucking car.'

I don't think I've ever heard him swear.

I laugh, then stop, head pounding …

ANA

… stomach lurching,
as wheels lift.
Airborne in a giant metal bird.
Yellow armband on my wrist.
Darwin shrinks,
into a smattering of buildings
clinging to the coast.
And then we're out over the ocean,
peering down
at nothing
but the endless chop
of waves.

JONO

I pull my laptop out as soon as the taxi drops us home. Make myself focus on the glare of the screen. Type in my password: *EagleEyes*, a nickname Mum used to call me when I was small.

I open the visit-request form for Wickham Point. It is still filled out from last time. Yesterday. Time has become a blur.

I change the requested visit date, and swap Aunty Minh's name for Dad's.

Then I email it off and wait.

I doze, slipping in and out of sleep.

I hear a tow truck arrive with Dad's car. Hear the driver's comment: 'How old's the Ford, mate? Practically an antique! Sure you don't want me to tow it to the mechanic? Don't think you'll get it running again in a hurry.'

Aunty Minh brings over some food – her cure for everything. But I can't stomach much.

Will calls with news, delivered in stunned, self-pitying tones. 'They're sending me away. Down south. To some boarding school called Geelong Grammar.'

'Shit.' I don't want to lose him. I don't want him to go. 'I thought your mum was cool with everything. She let us drink and smoke.'

'Only in our house, remember? And Dad never liked that rule anyway. Always said she was too soft. Now he reckons he's got proof.'

I feel lost, and he hasn't even left. Yet another person I love, gone.

I express my devastation in language he'll understand:

'You're a fucking moron, you know that?'

I hang up and sink back into bed.

When I open my eyes again, there's a new email in my account. Wickham Point Security.

Classification: IN CONFIDENCE
Dear Kenny and Jonathan Do,
Please be informed that Fatemeh (KIN014), Setareh (KIN014.1), Arash (KIN015) and Anahita (KIN016) are not in Wickham Point so your visit can't be facilitated. You are requested to contact Australian Border Force for their current contact details.

My heart drops into my feet.

I push myself up straighter, and yell, 'Dad!'

KENNY

The Ford appears to have finally died, so I get Phoung's number from Minh, then call and ask to borrow her car so I can get to work. She playfully says I can use it as long as I take her out for dinner to say thanks. I'm blushing as I agree.

I drive her gleaming SUV out to Wickham Point in the cool of early morning. The sun rises golden and full of promise. We're inching towards dry season now, and the days are uniformly perfect and clear. But inside I feel numb, picturing Jonathan's hopeful face as I left: 'This will be your last shift, right? You'll just find out about Ana, then you'll quit?'

It was hard to be honest. 'I can't afford to. Not until I find something else.'

I park Phoung's car and climb out. Light a cigarette and stand smoking in the car park.

My gaze falls on a security camera nearby, one of those smash-proof, black half-globes they use on street corners in the city. I wonder if I'm in range of it and if anyone is watching me now.

I stub my cigarette out, and urge myself to walk towards the staff entrance.

But my feet won't move. I don't want to go in. Don't want to work here at all.

I force myself to put one foot in front of the other.

Once inside, I pass the girl's – Anahita's – room.

There are cleaners already in there, scrubbing it down in case of new arrivals, I guess.

One of the cleaners has a broom. She brushes cobwebs from the corners of the ceiling, then runs it roughly around the long rectangular fluorescent light. A few flakes of white fall to the floor. I take a step inside and see a scattering of glow-in-the-dark stars on the tiles by my shoe.

The cleaner with the broom looks up at me. 'Everything okay?'

'Oh, yes, yes. Sorry. Just checking ...'

Just checking what? I don't even know myself.

I hurry on to the staff computer room.

JONO

Today I don't even have to ask.

'They moved her. In the night,' says Zahra.

I can see the deep well of fear in her eyes.

'Where to?'

'I don't know ... but people say Nauru ... they say Iranian women with babies are sent there ...'

I google images of *Nauru detention centre* online. It is a tiny island, as flat and round as a pancake. There are photos of green army-style tents in rows. People leaning on wire fences, staring bleakly out. Kids protesting with signs: *Jesus help us* and *Let us back to Aus*. Demountables on razed, bare earth.

The photos make me feel sick and sad and scared.

I send Ana a stream of messages, but get no reply.

Ana, I'm so sorry.

Ana, forgive me.

Ana, are you okay?

Ana, are you getting these messages?

Please, just let me know you're alright.

Ana, are you there?

ANA

KENNY

My heart sinks as I reads Anahita's mother's file. For a moment, I sit there, thinking it through. I know Jonathan won't be satisfied with just knowing where they are. He'll want to know if they're okay and what happens to them now.

I pull up the internal contact list and scan the names. I find a case manager called Eliza. There couldn't be too many of those.

I dial the extension. Hear a man's voice. 'Brad Summers.'

'Sorry. I was trying to call Eliza.' I check the name. 'Eliza Wood?'

'Ah. She's not working here anymore.'

'Why?' I know the question sounds unprofessional. 'Sorry, this is just … a colleague. From work. I needed to talk to her … about a client.'

Brad pauses, seeming to weigh this up. Then he says, 'Look, she's been stood down. Got too close to some of the detainees. You know how it is, the ones straight from uni never last long. Is there some way I can help?'

'No.' I thank him and hang up.

I walk slowly outside and see silhouettes on the roof. Those two Rohingya men must've climbed up there again. They're huddled under the eaves, making the most of the tiny sliver of shade. I remember Scott's instructions to ignore them, and start to walk on. But I can feel their eyes on me. Could swear they're watching me as I pass.

I stop and turn to look up at them, then raise my hand and wave.

They wave back but do not smile.

JONO

I get a job at KFC, and start to work there on the weekends and some days after school. It's greasy and unglamorous, and the shifts seem long. I like working with Mel, but we both miss Will. He texts me and Snapchats photos from Geelong Grammar every other day. But it's a strange new world of suit-like uniforms and rugby and frosty breath and freezing-cold early-morning rising. He feels far away.

I think about Ana every day. She still hasn't replied to any of my messages. I picture the devastated look on her face when I asked why she left Iran. I read case studies of Iranian refugees and wonder if any of their stories are like hers.

One day after work, Mel invites me back to her house. Her mum gives me a forced bright-red lipstick smile, and rushes around us in a flurry of floral dress, as she sets out drinks and a plate of baklava for us to eat. We scoff a few pieces, then play kick to kick with Mel's two brothers in the backyard. Her mum watches us from the kitchen with a slight frown.

I ask if we should explain that I'm not Mel's boyfriend. Her parents never knew about Will; she's not allowed to date. But Mel just laughs and says to let her mum sweat on it for a bit.

Mel's dad arrives home. He's a customs guy at the airport and regales us with a story from his work. 'I asked him to step to one side and you know what he said? Accused me of choosing to scan him 'cause he looks Middle Eastern! I told him it was random. I'm not racist – my wife's Greek! But of course he didn't believe me. Started going on about terrorism and how people always expect him to apologise for all the bloody insane Muslims in the world.'

Mel looks uncomfortable. 'Dad ... Jono went out with one.'

'What?'

'Jono went out with a Muslim girl at our school.'

Her mum raises a perfectly plucked eyebrow.

Her dad backtracks quickly. 'Oh. Well. She was probably alright. I'm not saying they're all bad.'

I eat another piece of baklava, then excuse myself and walk home.

KENNY

I lean the rusty ladder against the side wall of our house. Test it's stable, then start to climb. Heave my compact body up then over the edge of the flat corrugated iron roof. I scramble to stand, then look around.

The sun is beginning to set. The world seems bigger up here. Rounder. More open. Free.

I wonder if this is what the Rohingyas see. If they actually get a clear view out, beyond the grid of fence.

I hear a voice from below. 'Dad? What are you doing up there?'

I walk to the edge and peer down. Jonathan is wearing his KFC uniform. There's a bag on his back, and a cardboard box of chicken in his hands.

I wave him towards the ladder. 'Come up.' Then, as an

afterthought: 'Bring that chicken with you too.'

He looks amused but tosses his bag onto the ground and starts to climb. He passes the chicken up to me before hoisting himself, easily and swiftly, onto the roof.

He stands beside me. The sky is all around us, bursting with pinks and purples. The mango tree by the house dances as a handful of small birds alight on its branches. I watch as one cocks its head and angles its pointed black beak towards me.

Jonathan follows my gaze. 'Rainbow bee-eater.'

'You sure?'

'Pretty positive. I could look it up in the book.'

'Why don't you take a photo? Send it to your mum, just to check. I bet she'd know.'

He slides his phone out of his pocket and takes a snap. The birds take flight in a shimmer of gold and green and blue.

'You get it?' I ask.

'Yeah.' He fiddles with his phone. I hope he's following my suggestion and sending it to Roxanne.

I pull a piece of KFC from the box, and bite into it. Jonathan seems to be watching me for a verdict.

'It's cold,' I say. 'Still tastes good though.'

He takes a piece too. We stand side by side, savouring the salty, oily flesh.

I catch his eye and smile. 'Not bad, huh?'

He grins back at me. 'Not bad at all.'

ANA

We
spend
two months
back
on
Nauru.
It joins the
list
of
Things I Will Not Discuss.
Then we're moved
to Sydney
into community
detention.
Our designated house
is made of crumbling
white cement.
It isn't much,
but we're together
and it's ours ...
for now.
We're still not free.
But there are
no officers
and no fences
and we can eat what we want.
Maman starts watching *The Voice* again,
but barely talks.

Abdul is too scared,
and too scarred,
to go outside.
A neighbour gives Arash a trampoline.
Setareh learns to sit up.
Jamileh stops answering the emails I send to her on Nauru.
Zahra writes occasionally from Wickham Point.
She says Ponyboy still asks about me,
now and then.
But I don't
reply to his messages
or call.
I start a new school,
so close that I can walk.
Each morning,
I tie my koala shoelaces,
push the iPod headphones
into my ears,
and with beautiful ugly music
in my head,
I start again.

POSTSCRIPT

As of August 2017, there are over 400 people seeking asylum who, like Anahita, have spent time on Nauru or Manus Island and are now in community detention in Australia. According to current Australian law, this group of people will never be permanently resettled in Australia. The government also announced in August 2017 that they will no longer be entitled to housing or income support and will be forced to return to Nauru or Manus Island, or the country they fled, in six months time.

There are approximately 1200 people in immigration detention in Australia, including on Christmas Island, and a further 2000 refugees and people seeking asylum on Nauru and Manus Island.

ACKNOWLEDGEMENTS

First and foremost, I would like to thank the amazing Shokufeh Kavani, who acted as a cultural adviser for the writing of this novel. Thank you for sharing your knowledge, stories and positive energy. I feel very lucky to have had your involvement and feedback on the drafts.

Huge thanks to Natasha Blucher, refugee advocate extraordinaire, who acted as a consultant, answering endless questions over three years and rigorously ensuring the story was true to life, accurate and honest. Thanks also to Justine Davis and Richard Davis from DASSAN, Caz Coleman and Joan Washington from Melaleuca Refugee Centre, and Claire Hammerton from Chilout.

While this story is fictional, and Darwin High is not the actual high school that asylum seekers have attended in Darwin, I am grateful to former principal Trevor Read for his support in allowing me access to the school, which is wonderfully diverse and has a high number of ESL and refugee students. Special thanks to Sarah Calver for sharing her teaching experiences.

Between Us has been researched and written at a time when the *Border Force Act* has been in place. This law prevents people working with asylum seekers – including public servants, doctors, teachers and security workers – from speaking out about the conditions they witness in immigration detention centres. I am therefore not able to name everyone I interviewed for the novel.

Some wonderful people I am able to name (to varying extents) include Veronica M. Hempel, Mark Conden, Sarah P, Sara, Natalie, Mike and Justin. Thank you for your expert knowledge, which added rich detail and authenticity. Many asylum seekers and refugees were also extremely generous in sharing their stories. Thank you in particular to Nirvana Qasimi, Atefeh, Habib, M, C, M, M, S, A, S and A. I wish you freedom and every happiness.

Others I want to acknowledge include: Johanna Bell for her knowledge of birds, friendship and all-round creative support; Jess Ong and Sam Pickering for their tales of growing up in Darwin; Dave Ma for answering questions about living between two cultures and our time in high school; the Ladies Who Write – Miranda Tetlow, Kate Wild, Kylie Stevenson and Jen Pinkerton – for their insights and feedback along the way; Annabel Davis for reading the first draft and providing invaluable feedback, as always; Khia Atkins for her science-lesson expertise, Jessie Cole for her grant-writing support and wise emails; Sarah Klissarov for her extensive knowledge of Iran; Mark Goudkamp for putting me in touch with Shokufeh and Sarah; Jarvis Ryan for some great research contacts and helping me find time to write; and Jeanne Ryckmans for believing in the idea for this book when it was only a paragraph long. Samanti De Silva, I would've loved to have had your wise input once again – rest in peace.

Elizabeth Troyeur, you are a wonderful agent and ongoing source of enthusiasm, support and advice. Aviva Tuffield, your edit notes were meticulous, and your honest and intelligent feedback pushed me to make the story stronger. Thank you to Black Inc. for being my publisher once again. Fiona Wood, Alice Pung and Melina Marchetta, thank you so much for taking the time to read *Between Us* and for your kind words. Having this dream team endorse this novel is a definite career highlight.

It would have been extremely difficult for me to have had the time to write this book without financial support in the form of grants from the Australia Council for the Arts, and the Northern Territory Government through Arts NT.

Thanks also to Varuna Writers House for the Residential Fellowship, which allowed me two focused weeks in which to complete the first draft.

To my extended families – both Vietnamese and Australian – you enrich my life in so many ways. To my dad, Binh Dinh, and mum, Pip Atkins, for your unwavering love and support.

And, finally, to Louis, Rosa and Nina, for always lighting up the dark.

ALSO BY CLARE ATKINS

Rosie and Nona are sisters. *Yapas*. They are also best friends. It doesn't matter that Rosie is white and Nona is Aboriginal: their family connections tie them together for life.

The girls are inseparable until Nona moves away at the age of nine. By the time she returns, they're in Year 10 and things have changed. Rosie prefers to hang out in the nearby mining town, where she goes to school with the glamorous Selena and her gorgeous older brother, Nick.

When a political announcement highlights divisions between the Aboriginal community and the mining town, Rosie is put in a difficult position: will she have to choose between her first love and her oldest friend?

WWW.BLACKINCBOOKS.COM